A Thane of Wessex

Charles W. Whistler

Contents

A THANE OF WESSEX

BY

Charles W. Whistler

CHAPTER I. OUTLAWED!

The whole of my story seems to me to begin on the day when I stood, closely guarded, before my judges, in the great circle of the people at the Folk Moot of the men of Somerset gathered on the ancient hill of Brent. All my life before that seems to have been as nothing, so quiet and uneventful it was compared to what came after. I had grown from boyhood to manhood in my father's great hall, on the little hill of Cannington that looks out over the mouth of the river Parret to the blue hills beyond. And there, when I was but two-and-twenty and long motherless, I succeeded him as thane, and tried to govern my people as well and wisely as he, that I too might die loved and honoured as he died. And that life lasted but three years.

Maybe, being young and headstrong, I spoke at times, when the feasting was over and the ale cup went round, too boldly of the things that were beyond me, and dared, in my want of experience, to criticize the ways of the king and his ordering of matters--thinking at the same time no thought of disloyalty; for had anyone disparaged the king to myself my sword would have been out to chastise the speaker in a moment. But, as it ever is, what seems wrong in another may be passed over in oneself.

However that may be, it came to pass that Matelgar, the thane of Stert, a rich and envious man, saw his way through this conceit of mine to his own profit. For Egbert, the wise king, was but a few years dead, and it was likely enough that some of the houses of the old seven kings might dare to make headway against Ethelwulf his successor, and for a time the words of men were watched, lest an insurrection might be made unawares. I thought nothing of this, nor indeed dreamt that such a thing might be, nor did one ever warn me.

My father and this Matelgar were never close friends, the open nature of the one fitting ill with the close and grasping ways of the other. Yet, when Matelgar spoke me fair at the rere-feast of my father's funeral, and thereafter would often ride over and sup with me, I was proud to think, in my foolishness, that I had won the friendship that my father could not win, and so set myself even above him from whom I had learnt all I knew of wisdom.

And that conceit of mine was my downfall. For Matelgar, as I was soon to find out, encouraged my foolishness, and, moreover, brought in friends and bought men of his, who, by flattering me, soon made themselves my boon companions, treasuring up every word that might tell against me when things were ripe.

Then at last, one day as I feasted after hunting the red deer on the Quantocks, my steward came into my hall announcing messengers from the king. They followed close on his heels, and I, who had seen nothing of courts, wondered that so many armed men should be needed in a peaceful hall, and yet watched them as one watches a gay show, till some fifty men of the king's household lined my hall and fifty more blocked the doorway. My people watched too, and I saw a smile cross from one of Matelgar's men to another, but thought no guile.

Then one came forward and arrested me in the king's name as a traitor, and I drew my sword on him, telling him he lied in giving me that name, calling too on my men to aid me. But they were overmatched, and dared not resist, for the swords of the king's men were out, and, moreover, I saw that Matelgar's men were weaponless. He himself was not with me, and still I had no thought of treachery.

So the end was that I was pinioned from behind and bound, and taken away that night to where I knew not. Only, wherever it was, I was kept in darkness and chains, maddened by the injustice of the thing and my own helplessness, till I lost count of days, and at last hope itself. And all that time the real reason for my arrest, and for the accusation that caused it, never entered my mind, and least of all did I suspect that Matelgar, my friend, was at the bottom of it. Indeed, I hoped at first that, hearing of my trouble, he would interfere and procure my release, till, as I say, hope was gone.

It was March when I was taken to prison. It was into broad May sunshine and greenness that I was brought out by my surly jailers at last, set, half blind with the darkness of the prison, on a good horse, and so, with my hands bound behind me, led off in the midst of a strong guard to the place of my trial.

Then, as mind and feeling came back to me with the fresh air and springtime warmth, I knew the place we were leaving: It was the castle of a friend of Matelgar--and that seemed strange to me, for I had been hardly treated, seeing none save the men who fed me and saw that my chains were kept secure. Then I looked in the faces of my guards, but all were unknown to me. As I had not before been to that castle as a guest, I was not surprised, and I said nothing to them, for I had found the uselessness of question and entreaty when I spoke at the first to the jailers.

So, silently, we rode on, and the world looked very fair to me after the long grayness of the prison walls.

One who knows the west country, hunting through it as I have hunted, grows to love and recognize the changing shapes of every hill and coombe and spur of climbing forest on their sides, and so, before long, I knew we were making for the great hill of Brent, but why I could not tell. Then we crossed Parret river, and I watched a salmon leap as we did so; and then on over the level marshes till I could see that the wide circle on Brent top was black with swarming people. Often enough, as the cloud shadows passed from them, arms and bright armour sparkled in the sunlight among the crowd; and then I could have wept, having no arms or harness left me, for often when aforetime I rode free I would take a childish pleasure in seeing the churls blink and shade their eyes as I flashed on them, and would wonder, too, if my weapons shone as my father's shone as we rode side by side on some sunny upland.

Then, when we came under the hill of Brent, the hum of voices came down to us, for the day was still, and my guards straightened themselves in the saddle and set their ranks more orderly. But I, clad as I was in the rags of the finery I had worn at the feast whence I was taken, shrank within myself, ashamed to meet the gazes that must be turned on me presently, for I saw that we were going on up the steep ascent to mix with the crowd on the summit of the great knoll.

Now, by this time the long ride had brought back my senses to me, and I began to take more thought for myself and what might be meant by this journey. At first I had been so stunned and dazed by the release--as my removal from the dungeon seemed to me--that I had been content to feel the light and air play about me once more; but that strangeness had worn off now, and the consciousness of being yet a prisoner took hold of me.

My guards had ridden silent, either in obedience to command, or because a

Saxon is not often given to talk when under some responsibility, so that I had learnt nothing from them thus far. But as we turned our horses' heads up the steep, a longing at last came over me to speak, and I turned to a gray-bearded man who had ridden silently at my right hand all the morning and asked him plainly whither he was taking me, and for answer he pointed up the hill, saying nothing.

Then I asked him why I must be taken there, and, grimly enough, he replied in two words, "For trial", and so I knew that the Great Moot [i] was summoned, and that presently I should know the whole meaning of this thing that had befallen me. Then my spirits began to rise, for, being conscious of no wrongdoing, I looked forward to speedy release with full proof of innocence.

Then I began to look about me and to note the crowds of people whom the Moot had gathered. So many and various were these that I and my guards passed with little notice among those who toiled up the hill with us, the crowd growing thicker as we neared the edge of the first great square platform on the hilltop. And when we reached this, my guards reined up to breathe their horses, for Brent has from this first platform a yet steeper rise to the ancient circle on the very summit. Men say that both platform and circle are the work of the Welsh, whom our Saxon forefathers drove out and enslaved, but however this may be, they were no idle workmen who raised the great earthworks that are there.

All the many acres of that great platform were covered with wagons and carts, and everywhere were set booths and tents, and in them men and women were eating and drinking, having come from far. There were, too, shows of every kind to beguile the hours of waiting or to tempt the curious, for many of the people, thralls and unfree men, had taken holiday with their masters, and had come to see the Moot, though they had no part in the business thereof.

So there were many gaily-dressed tumblers and dancers, jugglers and gleemen, each with a crowd round them. But among these crowds were few freemen, so that I judged that the Moot was set, and that they were gathered on the higher circle that was yet before us to be climbed.

I had been on Brent once or twice before, but then it had been deserted, and my eyes had had time and inclination to look out over the wide view of hill and plain and sea and distant Welsh mountains beyond that. Now I thought nothing of these things, but looked up to where it seemed that I must be judged. I could make out one or two banners pitched and floating idly in the sunshine, and one seemed to have a golden cross at its stave head; but I could make out none of the devices on them, and so I looked idly back on the crowd again. And then men brought us food and ale, and at last, after some gruff talk among themselves, the guards untied my hands, though they left my feet bound under the saddle girths, and bade me help myself.

Nor was I loth to eat heartily, with the freshness of the ride on me, and with the hope of freedom strong in my heart.

Then we waited for an hour or more, and the sun began to slope westward, and my guards seemed to grow impatient. Still the crowds did not thin, and if one group of performers ceased another set began their antics.

At last a richly-clad messenger came towards us, the throng making hasty way for him, and spoke to the leader of our party. Then, following him, we rode to the foot of the great mound, and there dismounted. And now they bound my hands again, and if I asked them to forbear I cannot well remember, but I think I did so in vain. For my mind was in a great tumult as we climbed the hill, wondering and fearing and hoping all at once, and longing to see who were my judges, and to have this matter ended once for all.

We passed, I think, two groups coming down from some judgment given, and of these I know one contained a guarded and ironed man with a white, set face; and the other was made up of people who smiled and talked rapidly, leading one who had either gained a cause or had been acquitted. There were perhaps other people who met us or whom we passed, but these are the two I remember of them all. Then we gained the summit and stood there waiting for orders, as it seemed, and I could look round on all the ring.

And at first I seemed to be blinded by the brilliance of that assembly, for our Saxon folk love bright array and fair jewellery on arm and neck. Men sat four and six deep all round the great circle, leaving only the gap where we should enter; and right opposite that gap seemed the place of honour, for there were a score or more of chairs set, each with a thane thereon, and in the midst of them sat those behind whom the banners were raised. Near us at this end of the circle were the lesser free-men, and so round each bend of the ring to right and left in order of rank till those thanes were reached who were highest.

Before those stood some disputants, as it seemed, and I could not see the faces of the seated thanes clearly at first. But presently I knew the banners--they were those of Eanulf the Ealdorman, and of Ealhstan the Bishop. And when I saw the first I feared, for the great ealdorman was a stern and pitiless man, from all I had ever heard; but when I knew that banner with the golden cross above it, my heart was lighter, for all men loved and spoke well of the bishop.

It seemed long before that trial was over; but at last the men ceased speaking, and the thanes seemed to take counsel upon it; and then Eanulf pronounced judgment, and the men sat down in their places in the ring, for it was, as one could tell, some civil dispute of boundary, or road, or the like which had been toward.

Then there was a silence for a space, until the ealdorman rose and spoke loudly, for all the great ring to hear.

"There is one more case this day that must come before this Moot, and that is one which brings shame on this land of ours. That one from among the men of Somerset should speak ill of Ethelwulf the King, and plot against him, is not to be borne. But that all men may know and fear the doom that shall be to such an one, he has been brought for trial by the Moot, with full proof of his guilt in this matter, that Somerset itself, as it were, should pronounce his sentence."

Now, when the assembly heard that, a murmur went round, and, as it seemed to me, of surprise mixed with wrath. And I myself felt the same for the moment-- but then the eyes of all turned in a flash upon me-- and I remembered the accusation that had been brought against me, and I knew that it was I of whom Eanulf spoke. Then shame fell on me, to give place at once to anger, and I think I should have spoken hotly, but that at some sign from the ealdorman, my guards laid hold of me, and led me across the open space and set me before him and the bishop.

But as he with the others laid hands on me, that gray-bearded man, who had answered me when I asked my one question, whispered hastily in my ear, "Be silent and keep cool."

I would he were alive now; but that might not be. And I knew not then why he thus spoke, unless he had known and loved my father.

So I stood before those two judges and looked them in the face; and then one moved uneasily in his seat to their left, and my eyes were drawn to him. It was Matelgar, and, as I saw him, I smiled for I thought him a friend at least; but he looked not at me. Then from him I turned to seek the face of some other whom I might know. And I saw thanes, friends of my father, whom I had not cared to seek; and of these some frowned on me, but some looked pityingly, as I thought, though it was but for a moment that my eyes might leave the faces of those two judges before me.

Now, were it not that when I go over what followed my heart still rises up again in a wrath and mad bitterness that I fain would feel no more, I would tell all of that trial, if trial one could call it, where there was none to speak for the accused, and every word was against him.

And in that trial I myself took little part by word or motion, standing there and listening as though the words spoken of me concerned another, as indeed, they might well have done.

But first Eanulf spoke to me, bending his brows as he did so, and frowning on me.

"Heregar, son of Herewulf the Thane, you are accused by honourable men of speaking evil of our Lord the King, Ethelwulf. What answer have you to make to this charge? And, moreover, you are further charged with conspiring against him--can you answer to that charge?"

Then I was about to make loud and angry denial of these accusations, but that old guard of mine, who yet held my shoulder, gripped it tightly, and I remembered his words, so that in a flash it came to me that an innocent man need but deny frankly, as one who has no fear, and I looked Eanulf in the face and answered him.

"Neither of these charges are true, noble Eanulf; nor know I why they are brought against me, or by whom. Let them speak--there are those here who will answer for my loyalty."

Now, as I spoke thus quietly, Eanulf's brows relaxed, and I saw, too, that the bishop looked more kindly on me. Eanulf spoke again.

"Know you not by whom these charges are brought?"

"Truly, I know not, Lord Eanulf," I answered, "for no man may say these things of me, save he lies."

"Have you enemies?" he asked.

"None known to me," I told him truthfully, for I had, as my father, lived at peace with all.

"Then is the testimony of those against you the heavier," said the ealdorman.

And with that he turned to the bishop before I could make reply; and they spoke together for a while in Latin, which I knew not.

So I looked to my friend Matelgar for comfort, but he seemed to see me not, looking away elsewhere. And I thought him plainly troubled for me, for his face was white, and the hand on which his chin rested was turning the ends of his beard between his teeth, so that he bit it--as I had seen him do before when in doubt or perplexity.

As I watched him, the bishop spoke in Saxon, saying that it would be well to call the accusers first and hear them, that I might make such reply as was possible to me.

"For," said he, "it seems to me that this Heregar speaks truth in saying that he knows not his accusers."

Then Eanulf bowed gravely, and all the circle was hushed, for a little talk had murmured round as these two spoke in private.

And now I will forbear, lest the rage and shame of it should get the mastery of me again, and I should again think and speak things for which (as once before, at the bidding of the man I love best on earth) I must do long penance, if that may avail. For, truly, I forgave once, and I would not recall that forgiveness. Yet I must tell somewhat.

Eanulf bade the accusers stand forward and give their evidence; and slowly, and, as it were, unwillingly, rose Matelgar, my friend, as I had deemed him, and behind him a score of those friends of his who had kept me company for long days on moor and in forest, and had feasted in my hall.

Again that warning grasp on my shoulder, and I thought that surely either I or they had mistaken the summons, and that my defenders had come forward.

Then, as in a dream, I listened to words that I will not recall, making good those accusations. And through all that false witness there seemed to me to run, as it were, a thread of those foolish, boy-wise words of mine that had, and meant, no harm, but on which were now built mountains of seeming proof. So that, when at last all those men had spoken I was dumb, and knew that I had no defence. For no proof of loyalty had I to give--for proof had never been required of me. And a man may live a quiet life, and yet conspire most foully.

As my accusers went back to their seats there ran a murmur among the folk, and then a silence fell. The level afternoon sun seemed to blaze on me alone, while to me the air seemed thick and close, and full of whispers.

Ealhstan the Bishop broke the silence.

"The proof is weighty, and Matelgar the Thane is an honourable man," he said, sadly enough; "but if a man conspires, there needs must be one other, at least, in the plot. Surely we have heard little of this."

Then was added more evidence. And men proved lonely journeys of mine, with evasion of notice thereof, and disavowal of the same. Yet I thought that Matelgar the Thane knew of my love for Alswythe, his daughter, whom I would meet, as lovers will meet, unobserved if they may, in all honour.

Yet, as I listened, it was of these meetings they spoke, saying only that I had been able to concord whom I met, and where, though Matelgar must have known it. When that was finished, Eanulf bade me call men to disprove these things. And I could not. For my accusers were my close companions, and of Alswythe I would not speak, and I must fain hold my peace.

Only, after a silence, I could forbear no longer, and cried:

"Will none speak for me?"

Then one by one my father's friends rose and told what they knew of my boyhood and training; but of these last few years of my manhood they, alas for my own folly could not speak. What they might they did, and my heart turned to them in gratitude for a little, though Matelgar's treachery had seemed to make it a stone within me.

They ended, and the silence came again. It seemed long, and weighed on me like a thunderstorm in the air, nor should I have started had the whole assembly broken into one thunderclap of hatred of me. But instead of that, came the calm voice of Ealhstan the Bishop:

"Eanulf and freemen of Somerset, there is one who witnesses for this Heregar more plainly than all these. That witness is himself, in his youth and inexperience. What are the wild words a boy will say? Who will plot against a mighty king with a boy for partner? What weight have his words? What help can come from his following? It seems to me that Matelgar the Thane and these friends of his might well have laughed away all these foolishnesses, rather than hoard them up to bring before this solemn council. This, too, I hold for injustice, that one should be kept in ward till his trial, unknowing of all that is against him, unhelped by the counsel of any freeman, and unable to send word to those who should stand by him at his trial. Indeed, this thing must be righted, I tell you, before England is a free land."

At that there went a sound of assent round the Moot, and it seems to me, looking back, that that trial of mine, hard as it was to bear, was yet the beginning of good to all the land, by reason of those words which it taught the bishop to say, and which found an abiding place in the hearts of the honest men who heard; so that in these days of Alfred, our wise king, they have borne fruit.

Then Eanulf signed to my guards, and they led me away and over the brow of the hill, that the Moot might speak its mind on me. There my guards bade me sit down, and I did so, resting head on hands, and thinking of nought, as it seemed to me, until suddenly rose up hate of Matelgar, and of Eanulf, and of all that great assembly, and of all the world.

There was an earthquake once when I was but a boy, and never could I forget how it was as though all things one had deemed solid and secure had suddenly become treacherous as Severn ooze. And now it was to me as though an earthquake had shaken my thoughts of men. For, till that day, never had I found cause to distrust anyone who was friend of mine. Now could I trust none.

Then rose up in my mind the image of Alswythe, fair, and blue eyed, and brown haired, smiling at me as she was wont. And I deemed her, too, false, as having tricked me to meet her that this might come upon me.

Well it was that they called me back into the ring to hear my doom, for such thoughts as these will drive a man to madness. Now must I think for myself again, and meet what must be. Yet I would look at no man as I went towards the place of my judges, and stood before them with my eyes cast down. For I was beaten, and cared no more for aught.

Eanulf spoke; but he had no anger in his voice and it seemed as though he repeated the words of others.

"Heregar, son of Herewulf," he said, "these things have been brought against you by honourable men, and you cannot disprove them--hardly can you deny them. They may not be passed over; yet for the sake of your youth, and for the pleading of Ealhstan, our Bishop, your doom shall be lighter than some think fit. Death it might be; but that shall not pass now on you, or for this. But Thane you may be no longer, and we do confirm that sentence. Landless also you must be, as unworthy to hold it. Outlaw surely must he be who plots against the Head of law."

He paused a moment, and then said:

"This, then, is your doom. Outlawed you are from this day forward, but wolf's head [ii] you shall not be. None in all Wessex shalt harbour you or aid you, but none shall you harm, save you harm them. Go hence from this place and from this land, to some land where no man knows you; and so shall you rest again."

Now, had I not been blinded with rage and shame, I might have seen that there was mercy in this sentence, and hope also. For I had seen a man outlawed once, and given a day's start, like some wild beast, in which to fly from the hand of every man that would seek his life. But I was to be safe from such harm, and but that I must go hence, I was not to be hounded forth, nor was my shame to be published beyond Wessex. So that all the other kingdoms lay open and safe to me.

None of this I heeded; I only knew that my enemies had got the mastery, and that ruin was upon me. So I ground my teeth and was mute.

Then they cut my bonds and I stood free, but cared not. Nor did I stir from my place; and a look of surprise crossed Eanulf's face. But Ealhstan the Bishop, knowing well, I think, what was in my mind, rose from his seat, and came to me, laying his hands on my shoulders. I would have shaken them off; but be kept them there gently, and spoke to me.

"Heregar, my son," he said, and his words were like the cool of a shower after heat, to my burning brain, "be not cast down in the day of your trouble overmuch. There are yet things for you to do in this world of ours, and the ways of men are not all alike. Foolish you have been, Heregar, my son, but the Lord who gave wisdom to Solomon the youth, will give to you, if you will ask Him. Go your way in peace, and if you will heed my words, take your trouble to some wise man of God, and so be led by his counsel. And, Heregar," and here the bishop's voice was for me alone, "if you need forgiveness, forgive if there is aught by you to be forgiven."

Then I knew that the bishop, at least, believed in my innocence, and my hard heart bent before him, though my body would not. He laid his hand on my head for one moment, and so left me.

One of my father's old friends rose up and said:

"Ealdorman, he is unarmed. Give him that which will keep him from wanton attack, or from the wolves, even if it be but a thrall's weapons."

Eanulf signed assent.

On that they gave me a woodman's billhook, and a seax, [iii] such as the churls wear, and one thrust a good ash, iron-shod quarterstaff into my hands. Then my guards led me away from the assembly, and set my face towards the downward path. Once again the old man spoke to me with words of good counsel.

"Keep up heart, master. Make for Cornwall, and turn viking with the next Danes who come."

I would not answer him, but walked down the hill a little. Then the bitterness of my heart overcame me, and I turned, and shaking my staff up at the hill, cursed the Moot deeply.

So I went--an outlaw.

CHAPTER II. THE FIGHT WITH TWO.

Now whither I went for the next two hours I cannot tell, for my mind was heedless of time or place or direction--only full of burning hate of all men, and of Matelgar most of all. And though that has long passed away from me, so that I may even think of him now as the pleasant comrade in field and feast that he once was, I wonder not at all I then felt; for this treachery had come on me so unawares, and was so deep.

Wherever it was I wandered it took me away from men, and at last, when I roused myself to a knowledge again of the land round me, I was hard on the borders of Sedgemoor Waste; and the sun was low down, and near setting.

Perhaps I had not roused even then; but it came into my mind that I was followed, and that for some time past I had heard, as in a dream, the noise of footsteps not far behind me. Now, since I was in the glade of a little wood, a snapping stick broke the dream, and I started and turned.

Where I stood was in the shadow, but twenty paces from me a red, level sunbeam came past the tree trunks, and made a bright patch of light on the new growing grass beneath the half-clad branches. And, even as I turned, into that patch of light came two of Matelgar's men, walking swiftly, as if here at last they would overtake me. And, moreover, that sunlight lit on drawn swords in their hands; so that in a moment I knew that his hate followed me yet, and that for him the Moot had been too merciful in not slaying me then and there, so that these were on that errand for him.

Then all earth and sky grew red before my eyes, for here seemed to me the beginning of my revenge; and before these two knew that I had turned, out of the dim shadow I leapt upon them, silent, with that quarterstaff aloft. Dazzled they were with the sunlight, and thinking least of all of my turning thus swiftly, if at all. And I was as one of the Berserks of whom men spoke--caring not for death if only I might slay one of those who had wrought me wrong.

Into the face of that one to the left flew the iron-shod end of the heavy staff and he fell; and as the other gave back a pace, I whirled it round to strike his head. He raised his sword to guard the blow, and that fell in shivers as I smote it. Then a second blow laid him across his comrade, senseless.

Then I stood over them and rejoiced; and part of my anger and shame seemed to pass into the lust of revenge begun well. I knew the men as two of Matelgar's housecarles, and that made it the sweeter to see them lie thus helpless before me.

I knew not if they were dead yet, but I would make sure. So I leaned my staff against a tree, and drew the sharp seax from my belt.

Then came into my mind the words of my father, who would ever tell me that he is basest who would slay an unarmed foe, or smite a fallen man; and hastily I put back the seax again, lest I should be tempted to become base as men had said I was; for I hold treachery to be of the same nature as that of which my father warned me.

I took back my staff and leant on it, thinking, and looking at those men. They were the first I had ever met in earnest, and this was the first proof of the skill in arms my father had spent long years in giving me. So there crept over me a pride that I had met two and overcome them--and I unarmed, as we count it, against mail-clad men. Then I thought that Herewulf, my father, would be proud of me could he see this.

And then, instantly, the shame of what had led to this swallowed up all my pride; and with that thought of my father's loved and honoured name, my hard heart was broken, and I leant my head against a tree, and wept bitterly.

One of the men stirred, and I sprang round hurriedly. It was the second man, whose sword I had broken. He had been but stunned, and now sat up as one barely awake, and unaware of what had happened. I might not slay him now, but quick as I could I took off my own broad leather belt and pinioned him from behind. He was yet too dazed to resist. And then I took his dagger from him, and bound his feet with his own belt, dragging him away from his comrade, and setting him against a tree. There he sat, blinking at me, but becoming more himself quickly.

Then I looked at the other man. He was dead, for the end of the quarterstaff had driven in his forehead, so madly had I struck at him with all my weight.

And now, seeing that I was cooler and might think more clearly, it seemed to me that it would be bitter to Matelgar that out of his wish to destroy me should come help to myself. I needed arms, and now I had but to take them from his own armoury, as it were. Well armed were all his housecarles, and this one I had slain was their captain, and his byrnie of linked mail was of the best Sussex steel, and his helm was crested with a golden boar, with linked mail tippet hanging to protect the neck. And his sword--but as my eyes fell on that my heart gave a great leap of joy--for it was my own! Mine, too, was the baldric from which it hung, and mine was the seax that balanced it, close to the right hand in the belt.

As I saw that I began to know more of the plans of Matelgar--for it must be that my hall and all my goods had fallen into his hands, and this was the reward his head man had asked and been given.

And now I minded that this man had been one of those who gave evidence of my lonely rides and secret meetings. So he had been bought thus, for my sword was a good one, and the hilt curiously wrought in ivory and silver.

Then I made no more delay, but stripped the man of his armour, and also of the stout leathern jerkin he wore beneath it, for I was clad in the rags of feasting garb, as I have said, and hated them even as I threw them aside. The man was of my own height and build, as it chanced, and his gear fitted me well. So I took his hide shoes also, casting away my frayed velvet foot coverings into the underwood.

Now once more I stood clad in the arms of a free man and how good it was to feel again the well known and loved weight of mail, and helm, and sword tugging at me I cannot say. But this I know, that, like the strong man of old our old priest told me of, as I shook myself, my strength and manhood came back to me.

But now, whereas I had been haled from my feasting a careless boy, and had stood before my judges as an angry man, as I look back, I see that from that arming I rose up a grim and desperate warrior with wrongs to right, and the will and strength to right them.

So I stood for a little, and the savage thoughts that went through my mind I may not write. Then I turned to my captive and looked at him, though I thought nothing concerning him. But what he saw written in my face as it glowered on him from under the helmet bade him cry aloud to me to spare him.

And at that I laughed. It was so good to feel that this enemy of mine feared me. At that laugh--and it sounded not like my own, even to myself--the man writhed, and besought me again for mercy. But I had no mind to kill him, and a thought crossed me.

"Matelgar bade you slay me," I said, "that I know. Tell me why he has sought my life and I will spare you."

"Master," said the man hastily, "I knew not whom I was to slay. Matelgar bade me follow Gurth yonder, and smite whom he smote."

"It would have mattered not--you would have slain me as well as any other."

"Nay, master," the man said earnestly, "that would I not."

"You lie," I answered curtly enough; "like master like man. Tell what I bade you."

"Truly I lie not, Heregar," cried he, "for I love my mistress over well to harm you."

Now at that mention of Alswythe the blood rushed into my face, for I had held her false with the rest, and this seemed to say otherwise, unless the plot had been hidden from such as this man. But I would fain learn more of that, for the sake of the hope of a love I had thought true.

"What is your mistress to me?" I asked. "Ye are all alike."

I think the man could see well at what I aimed, for he spoke of the Lady Alswythe more freely than he would have dared at other times, nor would I have let him name her lightly.

"Our mistress has gone sadly since the day you were taken, master; even asking me to tell her, if I could, where you were kept, thinking me one of those who guarded you, mayhap. But I knew not till today what had chanced to you. Men may know well from such tokens what is amiss."

Hearing that, my heart lightened within me, for I saw that the man spoke truth. However, I would not speak more of this to such as he, and I bade him cease his prating, and answer plainly my first question, laying my hand on my seax as if to draw it.

"Gurth could have told you; master," he cried, "but he is dead. Matelgar held no counsel with me. I can but tell you what the talk is among the men."

"Tell it."

"Because Matelgar had taken charge, as he said, of your lands while you were away, and knowing well that in your taking he had had some hand, men say it is to get possession thereof; and the women say that, while you were near, the Lady Alswythe would marry no other, so that he had had you removed."

The first I had guessed by the token of the sword that I had regained. That last was sweet to hear.

"Go on," I said. "How came Matelgar to have power to hold my lands?"

"There came one from the king, after you were taken, giving him papers with a great seal thereon, and these he read aloud in your hall, showing the king's own hand at the end. So men bowed thereto, and all your men he drove out if they would not serve him, and few remained. The rest have taken service elsewhere if they were free."

So Matelgar was in possession, and now would be confirmed in the same. What mattered that to an outlaw? But I could have borne anything better than to think of him sitting in my place as reward for his treachery. This was evidence of weakness, however, in his case, that he should have tried to have me slain.

Now I had learnt all I needed, and more, in the one thing next my heart, than I hoped, if that were true--for still I could not but doubt the faith of all. Only one thing more I would ask, and that was if Matelgar bided in his own or my hall. The man told me that he kept in his own place.

"Now," said I, "I had a mind to leave you bound here for the wolves, but you shall take a message to your master."

On that the man swore to do my bidding, or, if I would, to follow me.

"Save your oaths," I said. "I have heard a many today, and I hold them as nothing. Take these cast rags of mine, and bear them back to your master. Give them to him, and then say to him whatsoever you will-- either that you have slain me and these are the tokens, but that Gurth was by me slain, and you must leave him and his arms here because of the wolves which you feared; or else you can tell him the truth, as it has happened, and see what he does to you. I mind how he hung up a thrall of his by the thumbs once for two days. He will surely take good care of one of two who were beaten by an unarmed man. But I think the lie will come easiest to your master's man."

Thus spoke I bitterly, and cut the belt which bound the man's arms, thinking all the while that he would never go back at all if he were wise. But he said he would go back and tell the lie, and I laughed at him.

It was dusk now, and though I feared not the man, I would play with him yet a little longer in my bitterness. So I bade him keep still, and stir not till I gave him leave. His feet were yet bound, and he would need an edge-tool to loose that binding. Telling him, then, that I would not run the chance of his falling on me from behind, I took his dagger and the seax they had given me, and stuck them in the ground a full hundred yards away, and then bade him, when I was out of sight, crawl thither as best he might and so loose himself.

The poor wretch was too glad to be spared to do aught but repeat that he would do my errand faithfully, and thank me; and, but for the sort of madness that was still on me, I must have been ashamed to torture him so. I am sorry now as I think of it, and many a man who has well deserved punishment have I let go since that day, fearing lest that old cruelty should be on me again, perhaps.

Then I turned and walked away, and even as I passed the weapons, I heard the low howl of a wolf from the swamp to my right. Far off it was, but at that sound the man cast himself on hands and knees and began to crawl in all haste to free himself.

Then I laughed again, and plunging deeper into the wood, lost sight of him.

CHAPTER III. BY BELL, BOOK, AND CANDLE.

I had never been into Sedgemoor before, and so went straight on as I could, only turning aside from swampy places while the light lasted. Then I must wait for the moon to rise, and I sat me down under an old thorn tree on a little rise where I could see about me. I had come out of the woods, and all the moor was open to the west and south so far as I could see. I knew that the place was haunted of evil spirits, and shunned at night time by all: but now I was not afraid of them--or indeed of anything, save the wolves. The terror of the man I had left had put that fear into my head, or I think that, desperate as I was, only the sound of a pack of them in full cry would have warned me. Still, I had heard no more since that one howled an hour ago.

Cold mists rose from the marsh, and in them I could see lights flitting. A month or two ago I should have feared them, thinking of Beowulf, son of Hygelac, and what befell him and his comrades from the marsh fiends, Grendel and his dam. Now I watched them, and half longed for a fight like Beowulf's. [iv]

At last the moon rose behind me, and I walked on. Once a vast shape rose up in the mist and walked beside me, and I half drew my sword on it. But that, too, drew sword, and I knew it for my own shadow on the thick vapour. Then a sheet of water stretched out almost under my feet, and thousands of wildfowl rose and fled noisily, to fall again into further pools with splash and mighty clatter. I must skirt this pool, and so came presently to a thicket of reeds, shoulder high, and out of these rose, looking larger than natural in the moonlight, a great wild boar that had his lair there, and stood staring at me before he too made off, grunting as he went.

So I went on aimless. The night was full of sounds, but whether earthly; from wildfowl and bittern and curlew, from fox, and badger, and otter; or from the evil spirits of the marsh, I knew not nor cared. For now the long imprisonment and the day's terrible doings, and the little food I had had since we halted on the hill of Brent, all began to get hold of me, and I stumbled on as a man in a bad dream.

But nothing harmed or offered to harm me. Only when some root or twisted tussock of grass would catch my foot and hinder me I cursed it for being in league with Matelgar, tearing my way fiercely over or through it. And at last, I think, my mind wandered.

Then I saw a red light that glowed close under the edge of some thick woodland, where the land rose, and that drew me. It was the hut of a charcoal burner, and the light came from the kiln close by, which was open, and the man himself was standing at it, even now taking out a glowing heap of the coal to cool, before he piled in fresh wood and closed it for the night.

When I saw the hut, it suddenly came on me that I was wearied out, and must sleep, and so went thither. The collier heard the clank of my armour, and turned round in the crimson light of the glowing coals to see what came. As he saw me standing he cried aloud in terror, and, throwing up his hands, fled into the dark beyond the kiln, calling on the saints to protect him.

For a moment I wondered that he should thus fly me; but I staggered to his hut, and I remember seeing his rush-made bed, and that is all.

When I woke again, at first I thought myself back in the dungeon, and groaned, but would not open my eyes. But I turned uneasily, and then a small voice spoke, saying:

"Ho, Grendel! are you awake?"

I sat up and looked round. Then I knew where I was--but I had slept a great sleep, for out of the open door I saw the Quantock hills, blue across the moor, and the sun shone in almost level. It was late afternoon.

I looked for him who had spoken, and at first could see no one, for the sun shone in my face: but something stirred in a corner, and I looked there.

It was a small sturdy boy of some ten years old, red haired, and freckled all over where his woollen jerkin and leather hose did not cover him. He sat on a stool and stared at me with round eyes.

I stared back at him for a minute, and then, from habit, for I would always play with children, made a wry face at him, at which he smiled, pleased enough, and said:

"Spit fire, good Grendel, I want to see."

Now I was glad to be kept off my own fierce thoughts for a little, and so answered him back, wondering at the name he gave me, and at his request.

"So--I am Grendel, am I?"

"Aye," said the urchin, "Dudda Collier ran into village in the night, saying that you had come out of the fen, all fire from head to foot, and so he fled. But I came to see."

"Where is the collier then?"

"He dare not come back, he says, without the priest, and has gone to get the hermit. So the other folk bided till he came too."

"Were not you afraid of me?"

"Maybe I was feared at first--but I would see you spit fire before the holy man drives you away. So I looked in through a crack, and saw you asleep. Then I feared not, and bided your waking for a little time."

"What is your name, brave urchin?' I asked, for I was pleased with the child and his fearlessness.

"Turkil," he said.

"Well, Turkil--I am not Grendel. He fled when I came in here."

"Did you beat him?" asked the boy, with a sort of disappointment.

"Nay; but he disappeared when the hot coals went out," I said. "And now I am hungry, can you find me aught to eat?" and, indeed, rested as I was with the long sleep, I had waked sound in mind and body again, and longed for food, and I think that finding this strange child here to turn my thoughts into a wholesome channel, when first they began to stir in me, was a mercy that I must ever be thankful for.

Turkil got up solemnly and went to the hearth. Thence he took an iron cauldron, and hoisted it on the great round of tree trunk that served as table in the midst of the hut.

"Dudda Collier left his supper when he fled. Wherefore if we eat it he will think Grendel got it--and no blame to us," remarked the boy, chuckling.

And when I thought how I had not a copper sceatta left me in the world, I stopped before saying that I would pay him when he returned, and so laughed back at the boy and fell to.

When we had finished, the cauldron, which had been full of roe deer venison, was empty, and Turkil and I laughed at one another over it.

"Grendel or no Grendel," said the urchin, "Dudda will ask nought of his supper."

"Why not?"

"By reason of what it was made of."

Then I remembered that a thrall might by no means slay the deer, and that he would surely be in fear when he knew that one had found him out. So I said to the boy:

"Grendel ate it, doubtless. Nor you nor I know what was in the honest man's pot."

Turkil was ready to meet me in this matter, and looking roguishly at me, gathered up the bones and put them into the kilns.

"Now must I go home," he said, when this was done, "or I shall be beaten. But I would I had seen Grendel--though I love warriors armed like you."

"Verily, Turkil, my friend," said I, "a stout warrior will you be if you go on as you have begun."

Thereupon something stirred within me, as it were, and I took the urchin and kissed him, for I had never thought to call one "friend" again.

Then I feared to let him go from me, lest the thoughts of yesterday should come back, as I knew they would, did I give way to them. So I told him to bide here with me till the village people came to drive away Grendel, and that I would make all right for him.

Then we went out of the little hut, and sat on the logs of timber, and he told me tales of the wood and stream and meres to which I must answer now and then, while I pondered over what I must do and where betake myself.

My outlawry would not be known till the people had got home from Brent, and then but by hearsay, till the sheriff's men had proclaimed me in the townships.

This place, too, where a man could slay roe deer fearless of discovery, must be far from notice, and I would bide here this next night, and so make my plans well, and grow fully rested. But always, whatever I thought, was revenge on Matelgar uppermost.

Now Turkil would see my sword, and then my seax, and try my helm on his head, laughing when it covered his eyes, and I had almost bade him come to my hall at Cannington and there try the little weapons I had when I was his size, so much his ways took from me the thought of my trouble. But that slip brought it all back again, and for a time I waxed moody, so that the child was silent, finding no answer to his prattle, and at last leant against me and slept. Presently, I leaned back and slept too, in the warm sun.

I woke with the sound of chanting in my ears, and the ringing of a little bell somewhere in the wood; but Turkil slept on, and I would not stir to wake him, sitting still and wondering.

Then out of the wood came towards the hut a little procession, and when I saw it I knew that I, as Grendel, was to be exorcised. But though I thought not of it, exorcism there had been already, and that of my evil spirit of yesterday, by the fearless hand of--a little child.

There came first an old priest, fully vested, bearing a great service book in one hand, and in the other a crucifix, and reading as he went, but in Latin, so that I could not know what he read. And on either side of him were two youths, also vested, one bearing a great candle that flared and guttered in the wind, and the other a bell, which now and then he rang when the old priest ceased reading be-tween the verses.

After these came the villagers. I saw the collier among the first, and his knees shook as he walked. Then some of the men were armed with bills and short swords, and a few with bows. All, I think, had staves. After them came some women, and I saw one who wept, looking about her eagerly.

They did not see me, for the timber pile was next the kiln and a little behind it; so that before they got near I was shut out from view for a time.

While they were thus hidden from me, they stopped and began to chant again, priest and people in turn. After that had gone on for a little time, Turkil woke and sat up, but I bade him in a whisper to be silent, and putting his finger in his mouth he obeyed, wide eyed.

Then the little bell gave a note or two, and the reading began, so near that I could hear the words, or seem to remember them as I know now what they were.

"Adjuro te maleficum Grendel vocatum diabolum--"

So far had the priest got when they turned the corner of the house, and I stood up. There came a shout from the men, and the exorcism went no further, for the old priest saw at once, as it seemed, that I was but a mortal. Not so some of his train, for several turned to fly, sorely fearing that the wrestle between the powers spiritual had begun, and, as one might think, lacking faith in their own side, for they showed little.

But Grendel or no Grendel, there was one who thought not of her own safety. That woman whom I had seen weeping gave a great cry and rushed at me, seizing my little comrade from my arms, for I had lifted him as I stood, and covering him with kisses, chided him and petted at the same time.

It was his mother, who hearing that her darling had wandered away from his playmates with the intention of "seeing Grendel" as he avowed, had dared to join the rest to learn what had been his end.

The old priest looked on this with something of a smile, and then turned to his people saying:

"Doubtless the fiend has fled, or this warrior and the child had not been here. Search, my children, and see if there be traces left of his presence, and I will speak to the stranger."

They scattered about the place in groups, for they yet feared to be alone, and the priest came up to me, scanning my arms as he did so, to guess my rank. My handsome sword and belt seemed to decide him, for though the armour and helm were plain, they were good enough for any thane who meant them for hard wear and not for show.

"Sir," he said, very courteously but without any servility, "I see you are a stranger, and you meet me on a strange errand. I am the priest whom they call the hermit, Leofwine--should I name you thane?"

I was going to answer him as I would have replied but yesterday morning --so hesitated a little, and then answered shortly.

"No thane, Father, but the next thing to it--a masterless man."

"As you will, sir," he replied, thinking that I doubtless had my own reason for withholding whatever rank I had. "We meet few strangers in this wild."

"I lost my way, Father," I said, "and wandered here in the night, and, being sorely weary, slept in this empty hut till two hours ago, waking to find yon child here."

Now little Turkil, seeing that I looked towards him, got free from his mother and ran to me, saying that he must go home, and that I must speak for him, as his mother was wroth with him for playing truant.

The woman, who seemed to be the wife of some well-to-do freeman, followed him, and I spoke to her, begging her to forgive the boy, as he had been a pleasant comrade to me, and that, indeed, I had kept him, as he said some folk were coming from the village.

Whereon she thanked me for tending him, saying that she had feared the foul fiend whom the collier had seen would surely have devoured him. So I pleased her by saying that a boy who would face such a monster now would surely grow up a valiant man. Then Turkil must kiss me in going, bidding me come and see him again, and I knew not how to escape promising that, though it was a poor promise that could not be kept, seeing that I must fly the kingdom of Wessex as soon as I might. Then his mother took him away, he looking back often at me. With them went the most of the people, some wondering, but the greater part laughing at Dudda Collier's fright.

I asked the old priest where the village might be, and he told me that it lay in a clearing full two miles off, and that the father of Turkil was the chief franklin there, though of little account elsewhere. He had not yet come back from the great Moot at Brent, and that was good hearing for me, for though he must return next day, I should be far by that time.

While we talked, the collier and two or three men came to us, telling excitedly how that the kiln was raked out, and that the cauldron was empty--doubtless the work of the fiend.

"Saw you aught of any fiend, good sir?" asked the priest of me.

Now I remembered the roe deer in time, and answered, "I saw nought worse than myself"--but I think that, had the collier known my thoughts, he would have fled me as he fled that he took me for. But that he was sore terrified I have no doubt, for it seemed that he neither recognized me, nor remembered what he was doing at the kiln when I came. Maybe, as often happens, he had told some wild story to so many that he believed it himself.

"Then, my sons," said the hermit, "the fiend finding Dudda no prey of his, departed straightway, and he need fear no more."

However, they would have him sprinkle all the place with holy water, repeating the proper prayers the while, which he did willingly, knowing the fears of his people, and gladly trying to put them to rest.

Then the collier begged one after another to bide with him that night, but all refused, having other things to be done which they said might not he foregone. It was plain that they dared not stay; but this seemed to be my chance.

The men had many times looked hard at me, but as I was speaking with the priest, dared not question me as they would. So having seen this, I said:

"I am a stranger from beyond the Mendips, and lost my way last night coming back from Brent. Glad should I be of lodging here tonight, and guidance on the morrow, for it is over late for me to be on my way now."

That pleased the collier well enough, and he said he would take me in, and guide me where I would go next day. The other men wanted to ask me news of the Moot, but I put them off, saying that I had not sat thereon, but had passed there on my way from Sherborne. So they were content, and asking the hermit for his blessing, they went their way.

Then the old priest took off the vestments which were over his brown hermit garb, and giving them to the youths who had acted as his acolytes bade them depart also, having given them some directions, and so we three, the hermit, collier, and myself, were left alone by the hut.

The hermit bade the collier leave us, and he, evidently holding the old man in high veneration, bowed awkwardly, and went to fill and relight his kiln fires.

And then the old priest spoke to me.

"Sir, I was brought here, as you see, to drive away an evil spirit, which this poor thrall said had appeared to him last night, and from which he fled. Now all men know that these fens are haunted by fiends, even as holy Guthlac found in the land of the Gyrwa's, [v] being sorely troubled by them. But I have seen none, though I dwell in this fen much as he dwelt, though none so worthy, or maybe worth troubling as he. Know you what he saw? for I seem to see that your coming has to do with this--" and the old man smiled a little.

Then I told him how I had come unexpectedly into the firelight, and that the man had fled, adding that I was nigh worn out, and so, finding a resting place, slept without heeding him; and then how little Turkil had called me "Grendel", bidding me "spit fire for him to see".

At that the old man laughed a hearty laugh, looking sidewise to see that Dudda was at work and unheeding.

"Verily," he said, "it is as I deemed, but with more reason for the collier to fly than I had thought--for truly mail-clad men are never seen here, and thy face, my son, is of the grimmest, for all you are so young. I marvel Turkil feared you not--but children see below the outward mask of a man's face."

Now as he said that, the old man looked kindly, but searchingly, at me, and I rebelled against it: but he was so saintly looking that I might not be angry, so tried to turn it off.

"Turkil the Valiant called me Grendel, Father. Also I think you came out to exorcise the same by name, for I heard it in the Latin. But that was a heathen fiend."

The hermit sighed a little and answered me.

"They sing the song of Beowulf and love it, heathen though it be, better than aught else, and will till one rises up who will turn Holy Writ into their mother tongue, as Caedmon did for Northumbria. Howbeit, doubtless those who were fiends in the days of the false gods are fiends yet, and if Grendel then, so also Grendel now, though he may have many other names. And knowing that name from their songs, small wonder that the terror that came from the marsh must needs be he. And, no doubt," went on the good priest, though with a little twinkle in his eye, "he knew well enough whom I came to exorcise, even if the name were wrong, had he indeed been visibly here."

So he spoke: but my mind was wandering away to my own trouble; and when I spoke of Sherborne just now, the thought of Bishop Ealhstan and his words had come to me, and I wondered if I would tell my troubles to this old man as he bade me. But, though to think of it showed that I was again more myself, something of yesterday's bitterness rose up again as the scene at the Moot came back, and I would not.

The priest was silent for a while, and must have watched my face as these thoughts hardened it again.

"Be not wroth with an old man, my son," he said, very gently; "but there is some trouble on your mind, as one who has watched the faces of men as long as I may well see. And it is bitter trouble, I fear. Sometimes these troubles pass a little, by being told."

The kind words softened me somewhat, and I answered him quietly:

"Aye, Father--there is trouble, but not to be told. I will take myself and it away in the morning, and so bear it by myself."

He looked wistfully at me as one who fain would help another, saying:

"Other men's troubles press lightly on such as I, my son, save that they add to my prayers."

And I was half-minded to tell him all and seek his counsel: but I would not. Still, I would answer him, and so feigning cheerfulness, said:

"One trouble, Father, I fear you cannot help me in. I have nought wherewith to reward this honest man for lodging and guidance--nor for playing Grendel on him, and eating his food to boot."

"Surely you have honest hands by whom to send him somewhat? or he will lead you to friends who will willingly lend to you?"

And I had neither. I, who but a few weeks ago could have commanded both by scores--and now none might aid me. None might call me friend--I was alone. These words brought it home to me more clearly than before, and the loneliness of it sank into my heart, and my pride fled, and I told the good man all, looking to see him shrink from me.

But he did not, hearing me patiently to the end. I think if he had shrunk from me, the telling had left me worse than when I kept it hid from him.

When I ended, he laid his hand on my shoulder--even as the bishop had laid his, and said:

"Vengeance is mine. I will repay, saith the Lord."

And I, who had never heard those words before, thought them a promise sent by the mouth of this prophet, as it were, to me, and wondered. Then he went on:

"Surely, my son, I believe you to be true, and that you suffer wrongfully, for never one who would lie told the evil of himself as you have told me. Foolish you have been, indeed, as is the way of youth, but disloyal you were not."

I was silent, and waited for him to speak such words again. And he, too, was silent for a little, looking out over the marsh, and rocking himself to and fro as he sat on the tree trunk beside me.

"Watching and praying and fasting alone, there has been given me some little gift of prophecy, my son; now and then it comes, but never with light cause. And now I will say what is given me to say. Cast out you are from the Wessex land, but before long Wessex shall be beholden to you. Not long shall Matelgar, the treacherous, hold your place--but you shall be in honour again of all men. Only must you forego your vengeance and leave that to the hand of the Lord, who repays."

"What must I do now, Father?" I asked, in a low voice.

"Go your own way, my son, and, as you were bidden, depart from this kingdom as you will and whither; and what shall be, shall be. Fighting there is for you, both within and without: but the battle within will be the sorest: for I know that the longing for revenge will abide with you, and that is hard to overcome. Yet remember the message of forbearance."

Then I cried out that I must surely be revenged and the good man strove with me with many and sweet words, till he had quieted the thought within me again. Yet I longed for it.

So we talked till the sun sank, and he must go ere darkness fell. But at last he bade me kneel, and I knelt, who had thought in my pride never to humble myself before mortal man again, till one dealt me my death blow and I needs must fall before him.

So he blessed me and departed, bidding me remember that at sunrise and midday and sunset, Leofwine, the priest, and Turkil, the child, should remember me in their prayers. And, for he was very thoughtful, he told me that he would take such order with the collier that he would ask nought from me, nor must I offer him anything, save thanks. And he spoke to him in going.

I watched him go till I could see him no more, and then, calling my host, supped with him, and slept peacefully till the first morning light.

CHAPTER IV. THE SECRET MEETING.

I woke before the collier, who slept across the doorway on some skins, and lay in his sleeping place for half an hour, thinking of what should be before me, and whither I would go this day.

And, thinking quietly enough now, I made the resolve to leave at all events my revenge that I had so longed for to sleep for a while--for the words of the good priest had bided with me, and moreover, I had some hope from his words of prophecy. So I would see how that turned out, and then, if nought came of it, I would turn to my revenge again.

So having got thus far, the advice of the gray-haired warrior seemed as good as any, for it was easy to me to get into West Wales, and then take service with the under-king until such time as Danish or Norse vikings put in thither, as they would at times for provender, or to buy copper and tin from the miners.

But then a great longing came over me to see Alswythe once more, and learn the truth of her faith or falseness. The man I had bound seemed to speak truth, though she was the daughter of Matelgar. Yet if she were child of that false man, I had known her mother well, and loved her until she died a year ago. And she was a noble lady, and full of honesty.

Now as safe a way as any into the Westland would be over the Quantocks, and so into the wilds of Dartmoor and beyond, where no man would know or care for my outlawry--if, indeed, I found not more proscribed men there than anywhere, who had fled, as I must fly, but with a price on them. And if I fled that way, it was but a step aside to pass close to Matelgar's hall.

It was the least safe path for me, it is true--for I had had a taste of what sort of reception I should meet with at his hands did he catch me or meet with me. But love drew me, and I would venture and see at least the place where the one I loved dwelt.

Having made up my mind to that, I was all impatience to be going, and woke the collier, saying that I must be afoot. He, poor man, started up in affright, dreaming doubtless that the fiend had returned, but recovered himself, making a low obeisance to me, quickly.

Then he brought out bread of the coarsest and cheese of the best, grumbling that the fiend had devoured his better cheer. And I, being light hearted, having made up my mind, and being young enough not to look trouble in the face too long, asked him if he had none of the roe deer left over?

Whereat he started, and looked terrified at me. Then I laughed, and said that Grendel had told me what was in the pot, and the man, seeing that I was not angry, began to grin also, wondering. Then the meaning of the whole business seemed to come to him, and he sat down and began to laugh, looking at me from under his brows now and then, lest I should be wroth with him for the freedom. But I laughed also, and so in the end we two sat and laughed till the tears came, opposite one another, and that was a thing that I had never thought to do again. At last I stopped, and then he made haste to compose himself.

"Master," he said, "forgive me. But if you were Grendel, as I think now, there is a great fear off my mind."

"I was Grendel, Dudda," said I; "but you must have a sorely evil conscience to be so easily frighted."

"Nay, master; but from week to week I see none, least of all at midnight, and mail-clad men never at all. I think I am the only man who fears not this marsh and what may haunt it."

"That you may never boast again," said I; "for scared you were, and that badly!"

"It is between you and me, master," said he, with much cunning in his look; "as I pray the matter of what was in the cauldron may be also--"

"Well, as for that," I answered, "I ate it, and was glad of it, so I will not inquire how it came there."

But I was glad to have this secret as a sort of hold over this man, for thralls are not to be trusted far, nor was I in a mood to put much faith in any.

After that we ate in silence, and when we had finished, he put a loaf and a half cheese into a wallet, and took a staff, and asked me to command him. I knew not what the hermit had told him, so asked how much he had learned of my errand.

"That you are on king's business, master, and in haste. Moreover that your errand is secret, so that you would not be seen in town or village on your way."

"That is right," I said, thanking in my mind the good hermit, whose ready wit had made things so easy for me; moreover it was truthful enough, for outlawry is king's business in all earnest, though not the honour this poor thrall doubtless thought was put on me.

Then I told him that I need ask him but to guide me beyond Parret river, on this side of Bridgwater, for after that the long line of the Quantocks would guide me well enough. It was all I needed, for once out of this fenland I knew the country well--aye, every furlong of it-- but I was willing enough to let him guide me through land I knew, that if ever he were questioned--as he might well be when my outlawry was known--his tale of my little knowledge of the country would make men think me some stranger, and so no blame would come on him for harbouring me.

So we started in the bright early morning, and he guided me well. There is little to say of that journey, but finding from the man's talk that the Moot rose not until the next day, I thought, with a lifting of my heart, how Matelgar would likely enough be yet there, and that I might almost in safety, unless he had sent word back concerning me to his men, go and try to gain speech of Alswythe.

Now it chanced presently that, looking about me, I seemed to know the lie of a woodland through which we passed, and in a little was sure we were in that glade where I fought my fight. And next, I saw my quarterstaff still resting against the tree where I had left it. The collier saw it too, and said that some forester was doubtless resting close by, seeming uneasy about the same. But I said that no question should be made of his presence in the wood, if it were so, and we came up to it. Then he started, and cried to me to look around.

My billhook, covered with new rust from the dew, lay where I had thrown it in stripping off my own garments to arm myself; but of the man I had slain only scattered bones were left. The wolves had devoured him.

When I saw that, I thought that this dead man might as well pass for myself-- Heregar, the outlaw. So I examined billhook and quarterstaff, and at last said I knew them. They had been given to one Heregar, who had been outlawed and driven from the Moot even as I stood to watch the gathering as I passed by.

"Then his outlawry has ended here," said the collier. "The wolves have devoured him."

"Just as well," I said carelessly. "Shall you take his staff and bill? They are good enough."

"Not I," said the man. "It is ill meddling with strange men's weapons, most of all an outlaw's."

"Mayhap you are wise," I said, and, casting down the things alongside the bones, went on.

Now I had looked all round, and saw that my old garments were gone, so that the man I had let go had at all events started away with them. But now I knew that the news of my death would soon spread, hard on the publishing of the sentence of outlawry, for the doings of an outlaw are of the first interest to those among whom he may wander. As it was, indeed, to my guide, who spoke so much thereof that I knew he would be full of it, and tell it to all whom he met. And when he told me he should go back through the town I was glad, for so Matelgar would have news of the same, confirming the tale of his man, though not accounting for his captain. Whereby he would be puzzled, and his life would be none the easier, for I knew he would dread my vengeance, though it might be hard for me to compass.

At last we crossed the river, and went a little way together into the woods beyond, till we came to the road which should lead the collier back to Bridgwater town. And there I made him give me directions for crossing the Quantocks, as though I would go by Triscombe--which I feigned to know not, save by name given for my guidance on my way.

I looked for him to ask reward, but he did not, and what the hermit had told him I could not say, unless he had promised him reward on his return. He made a low salutation before me, cap in hand, and I thanked him for his pains, saying that I would not forget him, as I was sure he would not forget "Grendel". And so we laughed, and he went away pleased enough, giving me the wallet of food.

Then was I left alone in the woodlands that had been mine to hunt through, for, holding our land from the king himself, I had many rights that stretched far and wide, which doubtless that Matelgar coveted for himself, and would now enjoy. And hard it was, and bitter exceedingly, not to turn my steps straight through the town, where men had saluted me reverently, to my own hall where it nestles under the great rock that looks out over my low meadows, and away towards Brent across the wide river. But that might not be. So I tried to stay myself with the thought of the hermit's prophecy, and plunging deep into the woods, crossed far back of my own place, until I could circle round towards Matelgar's hall.

And there I must go carefully, lest I should be seen and known by any; but the woods were thick, and none knew them better than I. These things come by nature to a man, and so I should not be proud that the very woodmen would own that I was their master in all the craft of the forest, as my father had been before me.

Now Matelgar's hall, smaller than mine, though as well built, or better, lay in that glen which runs down towards the level meadows of Stert point between Severn and Parret, north of the little hills of Combwich and Stockland, and almost under that last. And there the forest came down the valley--for it is not enough for me to call a combe--almost to the rear of the hall and the quickset inclosure around it.

It was afternoon and towards evening when I came here, and I bided in the woods a mile from the hall, in a safe place where none ever came, until I heard the horn which called all men in to sup. Then, when I judged that they had gathered, I struck towards the path that leads down to the hall, keeping yet under cover. One ran in haste towards his supper as I neared it, so I knew that perhaps he was the last to take his place, and that for an hour or two I was secure.

Now in this wood, and not so far from where I was, is a little nook with a fallen tree, and here Alswythe and her mother were wont to come in the warm evenings, and sit while the feeding in hall went on, so soon as they could leave the board. And there, too, I had met Alswythe often lately, sitting and taking pleasure in her company, till she knew that I would want no better companion for all my life.

This was just such an evening as might tempt her there, and I would at least have the sorrow of biding there alone for the last time. So I crept to that place very softly, and sat me down to think.

Maybe I had sat there a quarter of an hour when I heard a step coming, and that step set my heart beating fast, for it was the one I longed for. Then I feared to frighten her with sight of an armed man in her retreat, but before I could move, she came round the bend of the path that made the place private, and saw me.

She gave a little scream, and half turned to fly, for she was alarmed, not knowing me in my arms. And all I could do was to take off my helm and hold out my hands to her, for I could not speak her name in my joy.

Then she laid her hand to her heart, and paused and looked; and before I could step towards her, she was in my arms of her own will; so I was content.

Now how we two found ourselves sitting side by side presently, in the old place, I may hardly say, but so it was. And I forgot all about her father and the evil he had wrought, knowing that she had no part in it, or indeed knowledge thereof.

For when we came to talk quietly, I found that she had thought me dead, and mourned for me: for Matelgar had told her that he knew nought of me. And I would not tell her of his treachery, for he was her father, and so for her sake I made such a tale as I knew he was like to tell her, though maybe the truth would come sooner or later: how that secret enemies had trapped me, and had brought false charges against me, which none of my friends could combat, so skilfully were they wrought, and then how that I was outlawed, and must fly.

And hearing this she wept bitterly, fearing, and with reason, that I should not return.

Then I comforted her with the hermit's prophecy, saying nought of her father. And she, sweet soul, promised that Matelgar should tend my lands and hall well till the words of the holy man came true, and I might take them back from him. And then she added that sorely cast down and troubled had her father seemed when he rode back from the Moot that day, and doubtless it was from this. But how glad would he be to know me living, and even now would take me in and set me on my way, notwithstanding the order of the ealdorman!

Now when I heard that Matelgar was indeed returned, and so close to me, I knew not what to do or say: for all my plans that he should think me dead were like to be overthrown by the talk of this innocent daughter of his.

And she, seeing me troubled, would have me say what it was, and I found it hard to answer her.

At last I told her how even Matelgar dared not harbour or assist me, and cried out on my folly in bringing blame even on her, were my presence known. But she stopped my mouth, telling me most lovingly that the risk was worth the running, so that she knew me living again.

Then I said that, lest harm should come to her father, it were better to keep secret that I had been here. And that, moreover, those enemies of mine would doubtless track me till they knew me gone from the kingdom, so that were a whisper to go abroad that I had been seen here, it might be death for me.

"And for this," I added, "it is likely that Matelgar, your father, will have it spread abroad that I am dead, in his care for my safety. For so will question about me and where I am cease."

This I said lest she should deny when the news came, as it must, that this was so.

Yet she longed to tell her father that I was here; but at last I overpersuaded her, and she promised to tell none, not even him, that she had seen me, and for my sake to feign to believe that I was dead.

Then we must part. I told her my plans for going still westward to make myself a name, if that might be; and promised to let her have news of me, if and when I might, and in all to be true to her.

And she, brave girl, would try not to weep as I kissed her for the last time; and gave me the little silver cross from her neck to keep for her sake, telling me that she would pray for me night and day, and that surely her prayers, and those of the holy man and the innocent child would be heard for me, so that the prophecy would come true. And more she said, which I may not write. Then footsteps came up the main path, and I must go.

I heard her singing as she went back to the hail in the evening light, and knew that that was for my sake, and not for lightness of heart; and so, when her voice died away, I plunged again into the woods, making westward while light lasted.

CHAPTER V. THE VIKINGS ARRIVE.

Now after I had parted from Alswythe, my true love, I could not forbear a little heaviness at first, because I knew not when I should see her again. But there is a wonderful magic in youth, and good health, and strength, and yet more in true love requited, which will charm a man from any long heaviness. So before long, as I went through the twilight woodlands towards the mighty Quantock hills, my heart grew light within me; and I even dared to weave histories in my mind of how I would make a name for myself, and so return in high honour by very force of brave deeds done, deeds that should be spoken of through all the land. It is a strange heart in a youth that cannot, or will not, do the like for his future, and surely want of such thoughts will lead him to nothing great, even if it does not bid him sink to the level of his own thralls, as I have known men fall.

However, my heart was full of brave dreamings, always with the thought of Alswythe as my reward at the end; so that I began to long to start my new life, and went on swiftly that I might the sooner leave behind the land that was to be closed to me.

Night fell as I came to the mouth of the long combe that runs up under Triscombe where the road crosses, and to south of it, and I began to wonder how I should lodge for the night. Then I remembered a woodman's hut, deep in the combe, that would serve for shelter, keeping the wolves from me, as it kept them from the woodmen, who made it for the purpose --the place being far from any village, so that at times they would bide there for nights when much work was on hand. None would be there in Maytime, for the season for felling was long past.

So I found my way to the hut, and there built a fire, and then must, in the dark, grope for a flint wherewith to strike light on steel, but could not find one among the thick herbage. So I sat in the dark, eating my bread and cheese, and thinking how that I was like to make a poor wanderer if I thought not of things such as this.

However, I thought my wanderings would last no long time, and as the moon rose soon I was content enough, dreaming of her from whom I had parted so lately.

I will not say that the wish for revenge on Matelgar had clean gone, for him I hated sorely. But for me to strike the blow that I had longed for would be to lose Alswythe, and so I must long for the words of sooth to come true, that I might see revenge by other hands than mine. Then again must I think of hurt to Matelgar as of hurt to Alswythe, so that I dared not ponder much on the matter; but at last was fain to be minded to wait and let the hermit's words work themselves out, and again fall to my dreaming of great deeds to come.

Out of those dreams I had a rough waking, that told me that I was not all a cool warrior yet.

Something brushed by the door of the hut with clatter of dry chips, and snarl, as it went, and my heart stopped, and then beat furiously, while a cold chill went over me with the start, and I sprang up and back, drawing my sword. And it was but a gray badger pattering past the hut, which he feared not, it having been deserted for so long, on his search for food.

Then I was angry with myself, for I could not have been more feared had it been a full pack of wolves; but at last I laughed at my fears, and began to look round the hut in the moonlight. Soon I had shut and barred the heavy door, and laid myself down to sleep, with a log for pillow.

Though sleep seemed long in coming, it came at last, and it was heavy and dreamless, until the sun shone through the chinks between the logs whereof the hut was built, and I woke.

Then I rose up, opened the door, and looked out on the morning. The level sunbeams crept through the trees and made everything very fresh and fair, and a little light frost hung over twigs and young fern fronds everywhere, so that I seemed in the land of fairy instead of the Quantocks. The birds were singing loudly, and a squirrel came and chattered at me, and then, running up a bough, sat up, still as if carved from the wood it was resting on, and watched me seemingly without fear. Then I went down the combe and sought a pool, and bathed, and ate the last of the food the collier had given me. Where I should get more I knew not, nor cared just then, for it was enough to carry me on for the next day and night, if need be, seeing that I had been bred to a hunter's life in the open, and a Saxon should need but one full meal in the day, whether first or last.

Now while I ate and thought, it seemed harder to me to leave these hills and combes that I loved than it had seemed overnight; and at last I thought I would traverse them once again, and so make to the headland, above Watchet and Quantoxhead on either side, and then down along the shore, always deserted there, to the hills above Minehead, by skirting round Watchet, and so on into the great and lonely moors beyond, where I could go into house or hamlet without fear of being known.

Then I remembered that to seek help in the villages must be to ask charity. That would be freely given, doubtless, but would lead to questions, and, moreover, my pride forbade me to ask in that way. Then, again, for a man so subsisting it might be hard to win a way to a great man's favour, though, indeed, a stout warrior was always sure to find welcome with him who had lands to protect, but not so certainly with the other housecarles among whom he would come.

So I began to see that my plight was worse than I thought, and sat there, with my back to an ash tree, while the birds sang round me, and was downcast for a while.

Then suddenly, as I traced the course that I had laid out in my mind, going over the hunts of the old days, when I rode beside my father and since, I bethought me of one day when the stag, a great one of twelve points, took to the sea just this side of Watchet town, swimming out bravely into Severn tide, so that we might hardly see him from the strand. There went out three men in a little skiff to take him, having with them the young son of the owner of the boat. And in some way the boat was overturned, as they came back towing the stag after them, when some hundred or more yards from shore, and in deep water where a swift current ran. Two men clung to the upturned boat; but the other must swim, holding up his son, who, though a big boy of fourteen, was helpless in the water. And I saw that it was like to go hard with both of them, for the current bore them away from shore and boat alike.

So I rode in, and my horse swam well, and we reached them in time, so that I took the boy by his long hair and raised him above the water, while the man, his father, swam beside us, and we got safely back to the beach, they exhausted enough but safe, and I pleased that my good horse did so well.

But the man would have it that I and not the horse saved his son, and was most grateful, bidding me command him in anything all his life long, even to life itself, saying that he owed me both his own and the boy's. And that made me fain to laugh it away, being uneasy at his praise, which seemed overmuch. However, as we rode home, my father said I had made a friend for life, and that one never knew when such would be wanted.

Now this man was a franklin, and by no means a poor one, so now at last I remembered my father's words, and knew that I was glad to have one friend whom I knew well enough would not turn away from me, for I had seen him many times since, and liked him well.

I would go to him, tell him all--if he had not yet heard it, which was possible--and so ask him to lend me a few silver pieces in my need. I knew he would welcome the chance of showing the honesty of his words, and might well afford it. Thus would I go, after dark lest I should be seen and he blamed, and so make onward with a lighter heart and freer hand.

So I waited a little longer in the safe recesses of the deep combe until a great gray cloud covered all the tops of the hills above me, and I thought it well to cross the open under its shelter to Holford Coombe, which I did.

There I loitered again, hearing the stags belling at times across the hollows to one another, but hardly wishful to meet with them in their anger. I saw no man, for once I had crossed the highroad none was likely to seek the heights in Maytime. And I think that no one would have known me. For in my captivity my beard had grown, and my hair was longer than its wont; and when I had seen my face in the little pool that morning, I myself had started back from the older, bearded, and stern face that met me, instead of the fine, smooth, young looks that had been mine on the night of my last feast. But there were many at the Moot, which was even now dispersing, who had seen only this new face of mine, and I could not trust to remaining long unrecognized. None might harm me, that was true; but to be driven on, like a stray dog, from place to place, man to man, for fear of what should be done to him who aided me in word or deed, was worse, to my thought, than open enmity.

Now as night fell the clouds thickened up overhead, but it was still and clear below, if dark; and by the time the night fairly closed in, I stood on the heights above Watchet, and, looking down over the broad channel and to my left, saw the glimmering lights of the little town.

There I waited a little, pondering the safest way and time for reaching the franklin's house, for I would not bring trouble on him by being seen. All the while I looked out over the sea, and then I saw something else that I could not at first make out.

Somewhere on the sea, right off the mouth of the Watchet haven, and seemingly close under me, there flashed brightly a light for a moment and instantly, far out in the open water another such flash answered it --seen and gone in an instant. Then came four more such flashes, each a little nearer than the second, and from different places. Then I found that the first and one other near it were not quite vanished, but that I could see a spark of them still glowing.

Now while I wondered what this might mean, those two nearer lights began to creep in towards the haven, closer and closer, and as they did so, flashed up again, and answering flashes came from the other places.

The night was still, and I sat down to see more or this, knowing that they who made these signals must be in ships or boats; but not knowing why they were made, or why so many ships should be gathered off the haven. Anyway there would be many people about to meet them if they came in, and that would not suit me.

Then all of a sudden the light from the nearest ship flamed up, bright and strong, and moved very fast towards the haven, and the others followed, for first one light and then another came into sight like the first two as they drew near. I knew not much about ships, but it seemed to me as if lanterns were on deck, and hidden from the shore by the bulwarks, perhaps, but that being so high above, I could look down on them.

"If they be honest vessels," thought I, all of a sudden, "why do they hide their lights?" for often had I seen the trading busses pass up our Parret river at night with bright torches burning on deck.

What was that?

Very faint and far away there came up to me in the still air, for what breeze there was set from the sea to me, a chant sung by many rough voices--a chant that set my blood spinning through me, and that started me to my feet, running with all the speed I could make in the darkness to warn Watchet town that the vikings were on them! For now I knew. I had heard the "Heysaa", the war song of the Danes.

But before I could cover in the dark more than two miles I stopped, for I was too late. There shot up a tongue of flame from Watchet town, and then another and another, and the ringing of the church bell came to me for a little, and then that stopped, and up on Minehead height burnt out a war beacon that soon paled to nothing in the glare of the burning houses in the town. I could fancy I heard yells and shrieks from thence, but maybe that was fancy, though I know they were there for me to hear truly enough.

But I could do nothing. The town was too evidently in the hands of the enemy, and I could only climb up the hill again, and watch where the ships went, perhaps, as I had seen them come.

As I clomb the hill the heavy smell of the smoke caught me up and bided with me, making me wild with fury against the plunderers, and against Matelgar, in that now I might not call out my own men and ride to the sheriff's levy with them, and fight for Wessex as was my right.

And these Danes, or Northmen, whichever they might be--but we called them all Danes without much distinction--were the very men with whom I had thought to join when I won down to Cornwall.

One thing I could do, I could fire the beacon on the Quantocks. That was a good thought; and I hurried to the point where I knew it was ever piled, ready, since the day of Charnmouth fight two years agone.

I found it, and, hammering with the flint I had found in case of such a necessity as last night's, I kindled the dry fern at its foot to windward, and up it blazed. Then in a quarter hour's time it was answered from Brent, and from a score of hills around.

Now, as I stood by the fire, I heard the sound of running footsteps, far off yet, and knew they were the messengers who were bidden to fire the beacon. So I slipped aside into cover of its smoke, and lay down in a little hollow under some bushes, where I could both see and hear them when they came.

They were four in all, and were panting from their run.

"Who fired the beacon?" said one, looking round.

"Never mind," said another; "we shall have credit for mighty diligence in doing it."

"But," said the first, "he should be here."

Then they forgot that in the greater interest they had left, or escaped from, and began to talk of the vikings.

The men from two ships had landed, I learned, and had surprised the place; scarce had any time to flee; none to save goods. They mentioned certain names of the slain whom they had seen fall, and of these one was the franklin whom I was going to seek. There was no help for me thence now.

One man said he had heard there were more ships lying off; but they did not know how many, and I could see they had been in too great haste to care to learn.

Soon fugitives--men, women, and children--began to straggle in wretched little groups up the hill, weeping and groaning, and I knew there would soon be too many there for my liking. So I crept away, easily enough, and went out to the headland.

But I could see nothing on the sea now; and so, very sad at heart, I sought a bushy hollow and laid me down and slept, while the smoke of Watchet hung round me, and now and then a brighter glare flashed over the low clouds, as the roof of some building fell in and fed the flames afresh.

I woke in the light of the gray dawn, and the smell of burning was gone, and the sea I looked out on was clear again, for a fresh breeze from the eastward was sweeping the smoke, as I could see, away to the other hills, westward. But the town was gone--only a smoke was left for all there was for me to look down on, instead of the red-tiled and gray-thatched roofs that I had so often seen before from that place or near it.

Next I saw the ships of the vikings. They lay out in the channel at anchor, for the tide was failing. I suppose they had gone into the little haven as soon as there was water enough, and that those lights I saw were signs made from one to the other when that was so. There were specks near them--moving--their boats, no doubt, from the shore, bringing off plunder. The long ships themselves looked like barley corns from so high above, or so I thought them to look, if they were larger to sight than that, for that was their shape.

Now I had not thought that they would have bided when the beacons were lit; but would have gone out westward with this tide. And therefore I wondered what their next move would be, but expected to see them up anchor and go soon.

Waiting so, I waxed hungry, for nought had I tasted, save a few birds' eggs that I had found in Holford Coombe, since that time yesterday. Birds' eggs, thought I, were better than nought, so I wandered among the bushes seeking more. As I did so, by and by, I came in sight of the beacon on the hilltop, and looking up at it, rather blaming my carelessness, saw that but two men were there, tending it, and from their silver collars I knew that they were thralls. They were putting on green bushes to make a smother and black smoke that would warn men that the enemy were yet at hand.

When I saw that both the men were strange to me, I went up to them, as though come to find out news of the business. And they saluted me, evidently not knowing me. I talked with them awhile, and then shared their breakfast with them, glad enough of it. They had, however, no more to tell me than I had already learnt, beyond tales of horror brought by the fugitives of last night, which I will not write.

Those people had soon passed on, fearing, as each new group came up, that the enemy was on their heels. They had doubtless scattered into the villages beyond.

So the time went idly, and the sun rose, while yet the tide fell and the ships lay beneath us. Smoke, as of cooking fires, rose from their decks, and they were evidently in no hurry. Nor need they be. In those days we had no warships such as our wise king has made us since then, and none could harm them on the open water.

In an hour's time, however, there came a change over the sea. Little waves began to curl over it, and when the sun broke out it flashed bright where the wind came over in flaws here and there. Then from each ship were unfurled great sails, striped in bright colours, and one by one they got under way, and headed over towards the Welsh coast, beyond channel. The tide had turned.

"They are going," said I, with much gladness.

One of the men shook his head.

"They do but slant across the wind, master. Presently they will go about and so fetch the Wessex shore again, and so on till they reach where they will up channel."

We watched them, and while we watched, a man came up from the west, heated and tired out, and limping with long running as it seemed. And when he saw me he ran straight to me, and thrusting a splinter of wood into my hand, cried in a panting voice:

"I can no more--In the king's name to Matelgar of Stert--the levy is at Bridgwater Cross. In all haste."

It was the war arrow [vi]. No man might refuse to bear that onward. Yet--to Matelgar--and by an outlaw! But the man was beat, and the thralls might not bear it.

"Look at me; know you who I am?" I said to the man, who had cast himself down on the grass, panting again.

"No--nor care," he said, glancing at me sharply. "On, and tarry not."

"I am an outlaw," I said simply.

"Armed?" he said, with a laugh. "Outlaw in truth you will be, an you speed not."

"I am Heregar," I said again.

"Curse you!" said the man; "go on, and prate not. If you were Ealhstan himself, with his forked hat on, you must go."

"Heregar--my master's friend," cried one of the two thralls, "if it be true you are outlawed, as I heard yesterday, go and win yourself inlawed again by this."

Then I turned, and wasted no more time, running swiftly down the hill and away towards the spot where my enemy lay at Stert, and that honest thrall of my friend, the slain franklin's, shouted after me for good speed.

"Well," I thought, as I went on at a loping pace, "I can prove my loyalty maybe--but I have to bear this into the wolf's den--and much the proof will serve me!"

Then I thought that presently I would feign lameness, and send on some other. And so I ran on.

I struck a path soon, and kept it, knowing that, if one met and recognized me, the token I bore was pass enough--moreover, none might harm me, if they would, so that I was doing no wrong in being turned back, as it were, by emergency, from leaving the kingdom. Now, as I trotted swiftly along the track, there lay in my way what I thought was a stone till I neared it. Then I saw that it was a bag, and so picked it up, hardly pausing, shaking it as I did so.

It was full of money! Doubtless some one of the fugitives dropped it last night as they went in haste, hardly knowing they had it, perhaps. Well, better with me than with the Danes, I thought, and so bestowed the bag inside my mail shirt, and thanked the man who sent me on this errand. For now I felt as if free once more;

for with sword and mail and money what more does man need?

When next I came to a place that looked out over sea, I could no more spy the ships. They must have stretched far across to the Welsh coast. Only the two holms broke the line of water to the north and east up channel.

Then the thought came to me that the Danes were gone, and what use going further with this errand? But that was not my business; the war arrow must go round, and the bearer must not fail, or else "nidring" [vii] should he be from henceforward. So I went on.

Now, at last, was I but a mile or two from Stert, and began to wish to meet one to whom to give the arrow--but saw no man. I turned aside to a little cluster of thralls' and churls' huts I knew. There were no people there, and one hut was burnt down. Afterwards I heard that they had been deserted by reason of some pestilence that had been there; but now it seemed like a warning to do the duty that had been thrust on me.

Then at last I remembered the prophecy of the old hermit--and my heart bounded within me--for, indeed, unlooked for as this was, surely it was like the beginning of its working out.

Now would I go through with it, and on the head of Matelgar be the blame were I slain. Known was I by name to the messenger who gave me the arrow, and to those thralls, and known therefore would my going to Matelgar be.

Nevertheless, when I went down that path that I have spoken of, toward the hall, looking to meet with one at every turn, my heart beat thick enough for a time, till a great coolness came over me and I feared nought.

Yet must I turn aside one moment to lock into that nook where Alswythe and I had met, but it was empty. I knew that it must be so at that hour, but I was of my love constrained to go there.

Then I ran boldly round the outer palisade and came to the great gate.

CHAPTER VI. IN THE WOLF'S DEN.

There was only one man near it, and he sat on the settle inside, so that he could see out and in as he wished. Him I knew at once, and was glad, for it was that old warrior who had showed some liking for me at Brent.

He got up slowly as he saw a stranger stand in the gateway and came out towards me. Then he started a little and frowned.

"Rash--master, rash," he said, but not loudly. "This is no safe place for you," and he motioned me to fly.

Then I beckoned him out a little further and showed him what I bore in my hand. And he was fairly amazed and knew not what to say, that I, an outlaw, should have been sent on this errand, and more, that I should have come.

I told him, speaking quickly and shortly, how it had come about, and he understood that the man who gave me the arrow neither knew nor believed me.

"Master," he said, when I had done, "verily I believe that you are true, and wronged by him I have served this past two months. But of this I know not for certain, being a stranger here and little knowing of place or people. But this I know, from the man you sent back, that our thane sought your life against the word of the ealdorman, and, moreover, believes that you are dead. But by the arms you wear I can learn how that matter really went. Now, give me the arrow, and I will see to this --do you fly."

But I was bent on ending the errand, and said I would carry out the task, as was my duty, to the end. I would put the arrow with its message into Matelgar's hand, and bide what might come.

He tried to dissuade me, but at last said that he would not stand by and see me harmed, and for that I thanked him.

"Well then," he told me, "you have come in a good hour. Most of the men have gone out here and there to spy what they may of the Danes and their plans--if gone or not. Others are in the stables, and but one man sits at the door of the great hall, and he is of no account."

"Where is Matelgar?" I asked.

"I know not exactly; but do as I say and all will be well."

Then I said that his advice had saved me, I thought, when before the Moot, and I would follow it here.

"Then," he went on, "come you to the hall door and bide there while I go in and call the thane thither. He will stay by his great chair to hear your message, and I will stand by the man who keeps the door. Then, when you have given up the arrow, tarry not, but come out at once, and get out of this gate, lest he should raise some alarm. Then must you take to the woods quickly."

So he turned and went in before me. There were some twenty yards of court-yard to be crossed before we came to the great timber-built hall, round which the other buildings clustered inside the palisades. But there were no men about, though I could hear them whistling at their morning's work in the stables, for the idle time of the day was yet to come. Only a boy crossed from one side to the other on some errand, behind us, and paid no attention beyond pausing a little to stare, as I could judge by his footsteps. At any other time I should not have noticed even that, but now that I was in the very jaws of the wolf, as it were, I saw and heard everything. And all the while my heart beat fast--but that was not from fear, but for thinking I might by chance see Alswythe.

Yet I will say it truly, that thought of her had no share in bringing me on this mad errand, which might have ending in such fashion as would break her heart.

One man, as my guide had said, sat just inside the hall, but I knew him not. Since he had my hall and his own to tend, Matelgar must have hired more and new housecarles. This man was trimming a bow at the hearth, and did not rise, seeing that, whoever I might be, I was brought in by his comrade. The great hall looked wide and empty, for the long tables were cleared away, and only the settle by the hearth in the centre remained, beside the thane's own carved seat on the dais at the far end.

"Bide by the fire till he comes," said my guide, seeing that the man did not know me, and leaving me there, he went through a door beyond the thane's chair to seek him.

So I stood where the smoke rose between me and that door, waiting and warming my hands quietly, and as unconcernedly to all seeing as I could.

"Ho, friend," said the man, so suddenly that he made me start; "look at your sword hilt before the thane comes," and he pointed and grinned.

Sure enough, my sword hilt was not fastened to the sheath as it should be in a peaceful hall, but the thong hung loose, as if ready for me to thrust wrist through before drawing the blade. So I grinned back, without a word, lest Matelgar should hear my voice and know it, and began to pretend to knot the thong round the scab-bard. All the same, I was not going to fasten it so that I could not draw if need were, and only kept on plaiting and twisting.

Then I heard Matelgar's voice and footstep, and I desisted, and, taking the arrow from my belt, stood up and ready.

He came in, looking round, but not seeing me at first through the blue smoke, for as I knew he would, he entered by the door through which my guide had gone just now. So I waited till he stood with his hand on his chair, while the old warrior came down towards me.

Then I strode forward boldly up to the foot of the dais, and looking steadily a Matelgar, cast the arrow at his feet, saying:

"In the king's name. The levy is at Bridgwater Cross. In all haste."

He threw up his hands as one too terrified to draw sword--who would ward off some sudden terror--giving back a pace or two, and staring at me with wild eyes. His face grew white as milk, and drawn, and his breath went in between his teeth with a long hissing sound. But he spoke no word, and as he stood there, I turned and walked out into the courtyard and to the gate, going steadily and without looking round, like a man who has nothing either to keep or hurry him.

Three grooms, whom I knew, stood with an unbridled horse on one side, but they were busy and minded me not till I was just at the gate.

Then one said to the other, "Yonder goes Heregar, as I live!"

Then there came a cry like a howl of rage from the hall, but no word of command as yet, nor did either housecarle come out that I could hear.

Then I was at the gate, and as I passed it, turning sharp to the right, for that was the nearest way to the woods, I heard one running across the court.

When I heard that, instead of keeping straight on, I doubled quickly round the angle of the palisade. By the time I had turned it the man may have been at the gate, and would think me vanished. But now I ran and got to cover in a thicket close to the rear of the house. A bad place enough, but I must chance it.

I could hear shouts now from the courtyard. I looked round for a way to escape, but to reach the woods I had now a long bit of open ground to cover, and was puzzled. Then overhead I heard a bird rustle, and I looked up, and at once a thought came to me. The tree was an old, gnarled ash, and the leaves on it were thick for the time of year. Moreover, the branches were so large that surely in the fork I could find a hiding place. And being so close to the hall, search would be with little, if any, care.

So with a little difficulty I climbed up, and there, sure enough, found the tree hollow in the fork, so that if I crouched down none could see me from below, while, lying flat against a great branch, I could safely see something of what might be on hand.

I was hardly sure of this when men began to spread here and there about the place, but mostly going in the direction of the woods. I heard Matelgar's voice, harsh and loud, promising reward to him who should bring in the outlaw, dead or alive, and presently saw him stand clear of the palisading, about a bowshot from me.

He was red enough now, but his hand played nervously with his sword hilt, and once when men shouted in the wood, he clutched it. Clearly I had terrified him, and if he deemed me, as it seemed, a ghost at first sight, the token of the arrow had undeceived him, and little rest would he have now, night or day, while I was yet at large.

So I laughed to myself, and watched him till he went back.

Presently the men straggled in, too. One party, having made a circle, came close by me, and they were laughing and saying that the thane had seen a ghost.

"Moreover," said another, "we saw him cross the court slowly enough, and when we got to the gate--lo! he was gone."

Then one said that he had heard the like before, and their voices died away as he told the story.

Soon after this the horns were blown to recall all the men, and I knew that Matelgar must needs, even were it a ghost who brought the war arrow, lead his following to the sheriff's levy.

Aye, and the following that should be mine as well. The message I had brought should have been to me as a king's thane, and I myself should have sent one to Matelgar to bid him come to the levy, even as he would now send to the other lesser thanes and the franklins round about, in my place. The men were running out even now, north and west and east, as I thought of this in my bitterness, and I watched them, knowing well to whom this one and that must go in each quarter.

This was hard to think of. Yet I had stood in Matelgar's presence, and had him in my power for a minute, while I might have struck him down, and had not done so. And all that long night in Sedgemoor I had promised myself just such a moment, and had pictured him falling at my feet, my revenge taken.

But how long ago that seemed. Truly I was like another man then. And since that night there had been the wise counsel of the hermit, the prattle of the child, the touch and voice of my loved one, the thought of a true friend, and now the sore need of the country I loved. And, for the sake of all those things, I do not wonder that, as I saw Matelgar pale and tremble before me, the thought of slaying him never entered my head.

I will not say that I was much conscious of all these things moulding my conduct; but I know that since I took this message on me, and it seemed to me that the prophecy was on its way to fulfilment, I had, as it were, stood by to see another avenger then myself at work in a way that should unfold itself presently--so sure was I that all would come out as the hermit foretold. So it was with a sort of confidence, and a boy's love of adventure, too, that I had run into danger thus, while now that I had come off so well, my confidence was yet stronger. However, it would not make me foolhardy, for my father was wont to tell me that one may only trust to luck after all care taken to be well off without it.

Men came trooping in from the nearer houses and farms very soon, armed and excited. Often some passed under me, not ten paces off, and then I shrank down into the hollow. All spoke of the Danes as gone, but at last one said he thought he could see them, away by Steepholme Island, half an hour agone. Though it might be fancy, he added, for their ships were very low, and hard to see if no sail were spread.

But from all I gathered, the Danes were over on the other coast, and out of our way for the time at least.

Then I grew very stiff in the tree: but so many were about that I dared not come down. They were, however, mostly gathered in the open in front of the great gate, and only passers by came near me. It was some three hours after noon before they gathered into ranks at last, and the roll was called over by Matelgar himself, as he rode along the line fully armed.

When that was done, he put himself at the head, and they filed off up the road towards Bridgwater. I remembered that, when I was quite little, my father once had to call out a levy against the West Welsh, and then there was great cheering as the men started. There was none now--only the loud voice of the thane as he chided loiterers and those who seemed to straggle.

I began to think of coming down when the last had gone, but a few men from far off came running past to catch them up, and I kept still yet. Then a great longing came upon me to join the levy and fight the Danes, if fight there should be, and I began to plan to do it in some way, yet could not see how to disguise myself, or think to whose company to pretend to belong.

The place seemed very quiet after all the loud talk and shouting that had been going on. My father's levy had had ale in casks, and food brought out to them while they waited. But I had seen none of that here. Maybe, however, it was in the court-yard, I thought, and this I might see, if I climbed higher, above the palisading.

So I left my sword in the hollow, lest it should hamper me, and went up a big branch until I could see over just enough to look across to the great gate, which still stood open. Then I forgot all about that which had made me curious, for I saw two figures in the gateway.

Alswythe stood there, talking with my friend, as I will call him ever, the old housecarle, and no one else was near them.

My first thought was to come down and run to her; but I remembered that I could but see one corner of the court, and that many more housecarles might be at hand, and waited, not daring to take my eyes from Alswythe lest I should lose her.

They were too far off for me to hear their voices, nor did they make sign or movement that would let me guess that which they spoke of; but presently the old man saluted, and Alswythe went out of the gate.

Then my heart leaped within me, for I thought, and rightly, that she sought her bower in the wood. And so she passed close by me in going there, and I must not speak or move for fear of terrifying her.

But when she had gone up the path, I looked round carefully once or twice, and came down, and then, buckling on my sword again, looked warily out of the thicket, and seeing that none was near, crossed the open and followed her.

There I found her in her place as she had found me the other day, and soon once more we were side by side on the old seat; and she was blaming me, tenderly, for my rashness. Yet she knew not that it was I who had brought the arrow, and her one fear was that I had joined those Danes. And when I looked at her, I saw that she had been sorely troubled, and this was the cause, for she said:

"I knew that you, my Heregar, would not fight against your own land, and so they would surely slay you."

So will a woman see the truth of things often more clearly than a man. For that the vikings might call on me to fight my Saxon kin had, till last night, never crossed my mind, yet after Charnmouth fight it was like enough.

Then she asked what brought me here, and I told her that, seeing the burning of Watchet, I had a mind to join the levy, if I could, and so fight both for country and for her. That was true enough as my thoughts ran now--and surely I was not wrong in leaving out the story of the errand with the war arrow, for that would have told her of her father's lust for my destruction.

Then she wept lest I should fall, but being brave and thoughtful for my honour, and for my winning back name and lands, bade me do so if I could, cheering me with many fond and noble words, so that I wondered that such a man as I could have won the love of such a woman as she.

Now the time was all too short for me to tarry long: but before I went, Alswythe would bring me out food and drink that I might go well strengthened and provided. And as I let her go back to the hall, I asked her the name of that old warrior to whom she spoke, for it was he, I told her, who had tried to help me before the Moot.

And then I was sorry I had told her that, for she might ask him of the matter and hear more than was good for her peace of mind; but it was done, and nothing could recall it.

Yet she did not notice it then, but said his name was Wulfhere, and that he was a stranger from Glastonbury, as she thought, lately come into her father's service. She was going then, and I asked her to let me have speech with him, as I thought it safe, if he were to be trusted, for I needed his advice in some things.

She said she would sound him first, not knowing how he had seen me already, of course, and so went quickly away towards the hall.

What I needed the old man for was but to try to repair my slip of the tongue, and warn him of my love's ignorance of her father's unfaith to me; but as it fell out, it was well I asked to see him.

Presently he came to me. I had to slip into the bushes and lie quiet till I knew who it was, and when I came out he smiled gravely at me, shaking his head, yet as one not displeased altogether.

"Well managed, master," he said, still smiling, "but I knew not that you had so strong a rope to draw you hither."

Then I told him the trouble I was like to bring on Alswythe if he told her all that passed at Brent; letting him have his own thoughts about my reason for coming to Matelgar's hall, which were wrong enough, though natural at first sight, maybe.

He promised to be most wary, and I was content. Then I asked him how I should join the levy.

"Master," he said, very gravely, "this is like to be a matter of which we have not seen the end. Yon Danes are up channel, and, as I believe, lying at anchor by the Holms. It will not be their way, if, having gone so far up, they sack not every town on their way back-unless they are beaten off on their first landing. Now the country is raised against them, sure enough; but our levy is a weak crowd when it is first raised, and they are tried warriors, every one. Now they may go on up tide to the higher towns, or else they will be back here, like a kite on a chicken, before men think, and Bridgwater town will see a great fight, and maybe a burning, before tomorrow."

Then I said that the levy would beat them off easily enough; but the old warrior shook his head.

"I was at Charnmouth," he said, "when King Ethelwulf himself led the charge. And our men fought well; but it was like charging a wall bristling with spears. Again and again our men charged, but the Danes stood in a great ring which never broke, although it wavered once or twice, until we were wearied out, and then they swung into line and swept us off the field. Until we learn to fight as they fight, we are weaker."

Then I began to fear for Alswythe, and asked him what guard was left for the hall, and again he shook his head.

"Myself, and five others--not the strongest--and a dozen women, and three boys, thralls."

I knew not what to say to this; but the wise old man had already thought of a plan in case of danger. And in this, he said, I could advise him, for he was a stranger.

"Horses enough are left," he told me, "and if the Danes come to Bridgwater, and are not beaten off, I shall mount the Lady Alswythe and the women, and take them to a safer place. But whither?"

I told him at once of the house of a great thane beyond the Quantocks, easily reached by safe roads through the forest land, where Danes would not care to follow, and he thanked me.

Then he said that I might well try to join the levy; but that it was possible that it would be hard for me. And I told him that if I could not manage it I would join in the fight when no man would question me, and that seemed possible to both of us. But if the Danes yet kept away I knew I could wait in hiding, having money now, safely enough till they had gone and the levy dispersed.

Then came Alswythe back, bearing with her the things I needed. And Wulfhere begged her not to bide alone in the wood now, since robbers might be overbold now that the men were drawn off to the levy. That was good advice in itself; but I knew that he would have her near the hall, lest there should be sudden need for fleeing. She promised him, thanking him for the warning, and he left us.

Then she tended me as I ate, carefully, and never had there been for me so sweet a meal as that, outlawed and homeless though I was to the world. For her word was my law now, and my home was all in her love for me.

I think no man can rightly be held an outlaw who has kept law and has home such as that. For while he has, and loves those, wrong will he do to none.

It was Alswythe who bade me go at last, not for her own sake, but for mine, that I might go on my way to win my fair name back again.

CHAPTER VII. OSRIC THE SHERIFF.

Through the woods I reached Bridgwater town before the sun set, and looking down from the steep hill that overhangs the houses, I could see the market square full of men, shining in arms and armour, and noisy enough, as I could hear. But every one of the townsfolk knew me, and by this time also knew what had befallen me, so that as I stood there it seemed not quite so easy to win a way to the levy as before. The highways were yet full of men coming in, for from where I stood on the edge of the cover I could see the bend of one road, and straight down another. If I went on them I must walk like a leper, alone and shunned by all, with maybe hard words to hear as well.

While I thought of all this, there crept out from among the woods an old crone, doubled up under the weight of a faggot of dry sticks, who stayed to stare at me. I did not mind her, but of a sudden she dropped her bundle of wood, and I saw that it was like to be a heavy task for her to raise it again. So I turned and laid hold of it, for she was but six paces from me, saying:

"Let me help you, Mother, to get it hoisted again. Truly would I carry it for you for a while, but I must bide here."

"That must you, Heregar the outlaw," said the old woman coolly, without a word of thanks, and I thought my story and face were better known than I deemed. Therefore I must make the best of it.

"Well, Mother," said I, "you know me, and if you know me, so also must many others. But I want to join the levy, and fight if need be."

"Thereby knew I you to be Heregar," said she; "for none but he must stand here with the light of battle in his eyes and his hand clutched on his sword hilt and not go down to the Cross yonder, as the summons is."

Then I marvelled at the old dame's wisdom, though maybe it was but a guess, and asked her what I should do, seeing that she was wise, and the words of such as she are often to be hearkened to.

"It is a wise man," she answered, "who will take advice; but never a word should you have had from old Gundred, save you had helped her, as a true man should."

"Truly, Mother Gundred," I said, "I have no rede of my own, and am minded to take yours."

"Then, fool," she said curtly, "link up that tippet of mail across your face, go down to Osric the Sheriff himself, beg to be allowed to fight, and see what he will tell you."

I had forgotten that I could hook the hanging chain mail of my helmet across, in such manner that little but my eyes could be seen; but then that was never done but in battle--and I had never seen that yet.

"Thanks, Mother," said I, with truth, for I saw that I might do this. "This is help indeed."

"Not so fast, young sir," answered the crone; "Osric will not have you."

"How know you that?"

"How does an old woman of ninety years know many things? When you tell me that, I will say how I know that Osric will send you about your business; and that will be the best day's work he ever did."

Now I was nearly angry at that, for it seemed to set light store on my valour; but there seemed something more in the old woman's tone than her taunting words would convey, so I said plainly:

"Then shall I go to him?"

"Aye, fool, did I not tell you so?"

"But if it is no good?"

"Is it no good for a man who is accused of disloyalty to have witness that he wished, at least, to spend his life for his country? Moreover, there is work for you to do which fighting will hinder for this turn-- go to, Heregar, I will tell you no more. Now do my bidding and go, and never will you forget that you helped an old witch with her burden."

"Well, then, Mother," I said, hooking up the mail tippet across my face, "if I must go down into the town, surely I will carry that bundle."

"That shall you not," she answered, dropping it again, and sitting down on it. "Heregar the king's thane--the standard bearer--shall bend to no humbler burden than the Dragon of Wessex. Go; and Thor and Odin strike with you."

And then she covered up her face, and would look no more at me. I thought her crazed, maybe, but a sort of chill came over me as I heard her name the old heathen gods, and I thought of the Valas of old time, and knew how here and there some of the old worship lingered yet.

However, good advice had she given, showing me the way to try my fortune in the way I wished, and after that heathenish blessing I had no mind to stay longer, for such like are apt to prove unlucky; so I bid her good even, and went my way towards the town. After all, I thought, king's thane I was once, and may be again; and to bear the standard must be won by valour, so that, too, may come to pass. Whereupon I remembered the badger that scared me in the moonlight, and was less confident in myself.

Many were the questions put me as I passed into the marketplace of Bridgwater, but I answered none, pushing on to where I saw Osric the Sheriff's banner over a great house. Mostly the men scoffed at me for thinking that I should win more renown in disguise; but some thought me a messenger, and clustered after me, to hear what they might.

When I came to the house door, where Osric lay, it was guarded, and the guards asked me my business. I said I would see the sheriff and then they demanded name and errand. Now, I could give neither, and was at a loss for a moment. Then I said that I was one of the bearers of the war arrow, and though that was but a chance shot, as it were, it passed me in at once, for often a bearer would return to give account of some thane ill, or absent, or the like.

They took me to a great oaken-walled hall where sat many thanes along great tables, eating and drinking, and at the highest seat was Osric, and next him, Matelgar. This assembly, and most of all that my enemy should be present, was against me in making my plea; but as the old crone had said, I should be no loser by witness.

I waited till a thrall had told Osric that one of his messengers was here, and then they beckoned me to go to him. He shifted round in his chair to speak to me, but I was watching Matelgar, and saw his glance light on my sword hilt. Recognizing it, he grew pale, and then red, half-rising from his seat to speak to Osric, but thinking better thereof.

"Well; what news and whence?" said the sheriff, who was a small, wiry man, with a sour look, as I thought. Men spoke well of him though.

"The Danes lie off the Holms, sir," I said, for I would gain time.

"I know that," he answered testily; "pull that mail off your face, man; they are not here yet, and your voice is muffled behind it."

I suppose that the coming and going of messengers was constant, and indeed there came another even then, so the other thanes paid little attention after they heard my stale news, except Matelgar; who went on watching me closely.

I was just about to ask the sheriff to hear me privately, when Matelgar plucked him by the sleeve, having made up his mind at last, and drawing him down a little, spoke to him a few words, among which I caught my own name.

The sheriff looked sharply at me, twitching his sleeve away, and I saw that there was to be no more concealment; so I dropped the tippet and let him see who I was, saying at the same time:

"Safe conduct I crave, Osric the Sheriff."

Then a silence came over the thanes who saw and knew me, looking up to see what this new freak of mine was. And Osric frowned at me, but said nothing, so I spoke first.

"Outlaw I am, Osric, but I can fight; today I bore the war arrow--that one who neither knew nor believed me gave me--faithfully to Matelgar the Thane, who is here in obedience to that summons. And when I took it I was on my way out of the kingdom as I was bidden, but I turned back because of the need for a trusty messenger. Now I ask only to be allowed to fight alongside your men in this levy, and after that it is over-- if I live--I will go my way again."

That was all I had to say, and when I ceased a talk buzzed up among the thanes. But Matelgar looked black, and Osric made no answer, frowning, indeed, but more I think at the doubt he was in than with anger at me.

I saw that Matelgar longed to speak, but dared not as yet, and then he cast his eye down the hall, and seemed to make some sign.

Presently Osric said in a doubtful way, "Never heard I the like. Now I myself know not why an outlaw should not fight if he wills to do so.

"What say you, thanes?" he cried loudly, turning to those down the hall.

Instantly one rose up and shouted, "We will have no traitors in our ranks."

Then I knew what Matelgar's sign meant, for this was a close friend of his. On that, too, several others said the same, and one cried that I should be hounded out of the hall and town. Osric frowned when he heard that, and looked at me; but I stood with my arms folded, lest I should be tempted to lay hand on sword, and so give my enemies a hold on me. Matelgar himself said nothing, as keeping up his part of friend bound by loyalty to accuse me against his will.

As for the other thanes, they talked, but all the outcry was against my being allowed to join, and at last Osric seemed to be overborne by them, for voices in my favour were few heard, if many thought little harm of my request. But then the offer of the help of one man was, anyway, a little thing, and if he were doubted it would be ill. And I could see, as Osric would also see, that the matter would be spread through the levy by those against me.

Now as I thought of the likelihood of one of Matelgar's men spearing me during the heat of fight, I wondered if he feared the same of me, for I have often heard tales of the like.

Then Osric answered me, kindly enough, but decidedly:

"Nay, Heregar, you hear that this must not be. Outlaw is outlaw, and must count for naught. I may not go against the word of the Moot, and inlaw you again by giving you a place. Go hence in peace, and take your way; yet we thank you for bearing the message to Matelgar. Link up your mail again, and tell any man that you bear messages from me; the watchword is 'Wessex' for the guards are set by now, and you will need it."

As he spoke thus kindly Matelgar's face grew black as night; but he dared say no word. So I bowed to the sheriff and, linking up my mail, went sadly enough down the hall. It was crowded at one place, and there some friendly hand patted me softly on the shoulder, though most shrank from me; but yet I would not turn to see who it was, that helped me.

Now I have often wondered that no inquiry was made about my arms, and how I came by them; but what I believe is, that even then men began to know that Matelgar and his friends had played me false, but that they would not, and Matelgar's people dared not, say much. As for Osric, his mind was full of greater troubles, and I suppose he never thought thereof.

I passed out into the street, but now it was falling dark, and few noticed me. The men sat about along the house walls on settles, eating and drinking and singing. And I, coming to a dark place, sat down among a few and ate and drank as well for half an hour, and then passing the guards at the entrance to the town on the road to Cannington, struck out for Stert, that I might be near Alswythe, and wait for the possible coming of the Danes, and the battle in which I might join.

CHAPTER VIII. THE FIRES OF STERT.

I went along the highroad now, for it was dark, and few were about. Only now and then I met a little party of men hurrying to the gathering place, and mostly they spoke to me, asking for news. And from them I learned, too, that nothing had been seen, while daylight served, of the Danes. Once, I had to say I was on Osric's errand, as he bade me, being questioned as to why I was heading away from the town.

I could not see my hall as I passed close by its place, for the lights that ever shone thence in the old days, so lately, yet seeming so long, gone, were quenched. But I thought of a safe place whence to watch if the Danes came, where were trees in which I might hide if need were, as I had hidden this morning. This was on the little spur of hill men call by the name of the fisher's village below it, Combwich. It looked on all the windings of Parret river, and there would I soon know if landing was to be made for attack on Bridgwater. But I thought it likely that there would be an outpost of our men there for the same reason, and going thither went carefully.

Sure enough there was a little watchfire and half a dozen men round it on the best outlook, and so I passed on still further, following round the spur of hill till I came to where the land overlooks the whole long tongue of Stert Point. That would do as well for me, I thought, and choosing, as best I could in the dark, a tree into which I knew by remembrance that I might easily get, I sat down at its foot, looking seaward.

Now by this time the tide, which runs very strong and swiftly, must be flowing again, and I thought that most likely the Danes, having anchored during the ebb, would go on up channel with it, and that therefore I might have to hang about here for days before they landed, even were they to land at all. And this I had heard said many times by the men of the levy, some, indeed, saying that they might as well go home again.

But I should do as well here as anywhere, or better, since, while Matelgar was away, I might yet see Alswythe again; though that, after my repulse by the sheriff, or perhaps I should rather say by his advisers, I thought not of trying yet. It would but be another parting. Still, I might find old Wulfhere, and send her messages by him before setting out westward again.

Almost was I dozing, for the day had been very long, when from close to Stert came that which roused me completely, setting my heart beating.

It was a bright flash of light from close inshore, on the Severn side of the tongue, followed by answering flashes, just as I had seen them at Watchet. But now the flashes came and went out instantly, for I was no longer looking down on the ship's decks as then.

Well was it that I had seen this before from Quantock heights; for I knew that once again the Danes were landing, and that the peril was close at hand.

Then at once I knew the terrible danger of Alswythe, for Matelgar's was the first hall that would be burnt.

My first thought was to hasten thither and alarm Wulfhere, and then to hurry back to that outpost I had passed half a mile away, for the country danger must be thought of too.

Then a better thought than either came to me. If it was, as it must be, barely half tide, the Danes would find mud between them and shore, too deep to cross, and must wait till the ships could come up to land, or until there was water enough to float their boats. I had an hour or more yet before they set foot on shore.

Moreover, I would find out if landing was indeed meant, or if these were but signals for keeping channel on the outward course.

So across the level meadows of Stert I ran my best, right towards the place where I had seen the light, which was at the top, as it were, of the wedge that Stert makes between the waters of Parret and the greater Severn Sea. There are high banks along the shore to keep out the spring tides, and under these I could watch in safety, unseen. Three fishers' huts were there only; but these I knew would be deserted for fear of the Danes.

So I found them, and then, creeping up the bank, I stood still and peered out into the darkness. Yet it was not so dark on the water (which gleamed a little in the tide swirls here and there beyond half a mile of mud, black as pitch in contrast) but that I could make out at last six long black ships, lying as it seemed on the edge of the ooze. And I could hear, too, hoarse voices crying out on board of them, and now and then the rattle of anchor chains or the like, when the wind blew from them to me.

And ever those ships crept nearer to me, so that I knew they were edging up to the land as the tide rose.

That learnt, I knew what to do. I ran to the nearest fishers' hut, and pulled handfuls of the thatch from under the eaves, piling it to windward against the wooden walls. Then I fired the heap, and it blazed up bright and strong, and at once came a great howl of rage from the ships, plain to be heard, for they knew that now they might not land unknown.

So had I warned Osric the Sheriff, and that matter was out of my hands. And, moreover, Wulfhere, being an old and tried warrior, would be warned as well.

That, however, I would see to myself, and, if I could, I would aid him in getting Alswythe into a place of safety. So I ran back, bending my steps now towards her father's hall, up the roadway, if one might so call the track through the marshland that led thither.

Just at the foot of the hill I met three men of the outpost, who were hurrying down to see what my fire meant. They challenged me, halting with levelled spears across the track. Then was I glad of the password, and answered by giving it.

"Right!" said the man who seemed to be the leader. "What news?"

I told him quickly, bidding him waste no time, but hurry back and tell the sheriff that the Danes would be ashore in half an hour. I spoke as I was wont to speak when I was a thane, forgetting in the dire need of the moment that I was an outlaw now, and the man was offended thereat.

"Who are you to command me thus?" he said shortly.

"Heregar, the thane of Cannington." said I, still only anxious that he should go quickly.

"Heard one ever the like!" said the man, and then I remembered.

I looked round at my fire. Two huts were burning now, very brightly, for the wind fanned the flames.

"Saw you ever the like?" I said, and pointed. "Now, will you go?"

The bright light shone on a row of flashing, gilded dragon heads on the ships' stems--on lines of starlike specks beyond them, which were helms and mail coats-- and on lines again of smaller stars above, which were spear points.

"Holy saints!" cried the man, adding a greater oath yet; "be you Heregar the outlaw or no, truth you tell, and well have you done. Let us begone, men!"

And with that those three leapt away into the darkness up the hill, leaving me to follow if I listed.

That was not my way, however, and I ran on to Matelgar's hall.

One stood at the gate. It was Wulfhere. Inside I heard the trampling of horses, and knew that they would be ready in time. Wulfhere laid hand on sword as I came up, doubting if I were not a Dane, but I cried to him who I was, and he came out a step or two to me, asking for news.

And when I told him what I had seen and done, he, too, said I had done well, and that I had saved Alswythe, if not many more. Also, that he had sent a man to tell Matelgar of his plans. Then he told me that even now the horses were ready, and that he was about to abandon the place, going to the house of that thane of whom I had told him. And I said that I would go some way with him, and then return to join the levy, making known my ill-luck with Osric.

"Ho!" said he; "it was well he sent you away, as it seems to me."

That was the word of the old crone, I remembered, that it should be so.

Then came a soft touch on my arm, and on turning I saw Alswythe standing by me, wrapped in a long cloak, and ready. And neither I nor she thought shame that I should lay my arm round her, and kiss her there, with the grim old housecarle standing by and pretending to look out over Stert, where the light of my fires shone above the trees.

"Heregar, my loved one, what does it all mean?" she said, trembling a little. "Have they come?"

I folded my arm more closely round her, and would have answered, but that Wulfhere did so for me.

"Aye, lady, and it is to Heregar that we owe our safety, for he has been down to Stert and warned us all."

At that my love crept closer to me, as it were to thank me. Then she said:

"Will there be fighting? And will my father have to fight?"

"Aye, lady," said Wulfhere again, "as a good Saxon should."

"Must I go from here?" she asked again; and I told her that the house would be burnt, maybe, in an hour or so.

At that she shivered, and tried not to weep, being very brave.

"Where must we go?" she said, with a little tremble in her voice.

I told her where we would take her, and then she cried out that she must bide near at hand lest her father should be hurt, and none to tend him.

And Wulfhere and I tried a little to overpersuade her, but then a groom came to say that all was ready.

And, truly, no time must be lost, if we would get off safely.

Then I said that it would be safe to go to Bridgwater, for then we should be behind the levy, and that the Danes must cut through that before reaching us. And to that Wulfhere agreed, for I knew he would rather be swinging his sword against the Danes at Stert than flying through the woods of the Quantocks.

Alswythe thanked me, without words indeed, and then in a few minutes she was mounted, and we were going up towards the high road to Bridgwater. We had twelve horses, and on them were the women of the house, bearing what valuables they might, as Wulfhere had bade them. One horse carried two women, but they were a light burden, and we had no such terrible haste to make, seeing that every moment brought us nearer the levy. There were the men and boys as well, but they led the beasts.

Now when we reached the high road, some half mile away, suddenly Alswythe reined up her horse, by which I walked, giving a little cry, and I asked what it was.

Then she said, sobbing a little, that she would her cows were driven out into the forest where they were wont to feed, lest the cruel Danes should get them. And to please her I think I should myself have gone back, but that Wulfhere called one of the men, who, it seemed, was the cowherd, bidding him return and do this, if the Danes were not coming yet. Glad enough was I to hear the man say that he had done it already --"for no Dane should grow fat on beasts of his tending, and they were a mile off by now."

So we went on, and every minute I looked to meet our levy advancing. But the moon rose, and shone on no line of glancing armour that I longed for, and Wulfhere growled to himself as he went. I would have asked him many questions, but would not leave Alswythe, lest she should be alarmed. And all the way, as we went, I told her of what had befallen me with Osric, saying only that her father was there, but had not been able to speak for me. And I told her of the old crone's words, which she thought would surely come true, all of them, as they had begun to do so.

It is a long five miles from Matelgar's place to the town, and we could only travel at a foot's pace. But still we met no force. Indeed, until we were just a half mile thence, we saw no one. Then we met a picket, who, seeing we were fugitives, let us go on unchallenged.

But Wulfhere stopped and questioned the men, and got no pleasant answer as it seemed, for he caught us up growling, coming alongside of me, and saying--for Alswythe could not know the ways of war--that they would attack with morning light. But I felt only too keenly, though I knew so little, that to fight the Danes when they had their foot firmly ashore, was a harder matter than to meet them but just landed.

We were so close to the town now that I asked Alswythe where she would be taken. Already we were passing groups of fugitives from the nearer country, and the town would be full of them, to say nothing of the men of the levy.

She thought a little, and then asked me if she might not go to her father, wherever he was. But I told her that he was but a guest of Osric, as it seemed. Then she said that she would go to her aunt, who was the prioress of the White Nuns, and bide in the nunnery walls till all was safe. And that seemed a good plan, both to me and Wulfhere, for it would--though this we said not to Alswythe--set us free to fight, as there we might not come, and she would be safe without us.

Then I told Wulfhere how we could reach that house without going through the crowded town, and so turned to the right, skirting round in the quiet lanes.

The gray dawn began to break as we saw the nunnery before us, and it was very cold. But Alswythe pointed to a crimson glow behind us, as we topped the last rise, saying that the sun would be up soon.

Wulfhere and I looked at each other. That glow was not in the east, but shone from Matelgar's hall--in flames.

And then we feigned cheerfulness, and said that it would be so; and Alswythe smiled on me, though she was pale and overwrought with the terror she would not show, and the long, dark, and cold journey.

We came to the nunnery gate and knocked; and the old portress looked out of the wicket and asked our business, frightened at the glint of mail she saw. But Alswythe's voice she knew well, as she answered, begging lodging for herself and her maidens, till this trouble was over.

It was no new thing for a lady of rank to come into that quiet retreat with her train when on a journey; and after a little time, while the portress told the prioress, the doors were thrown open, and we rode into the great courtyard, where torches burnt in the dim gray morning light.

Then came the prioress, mother's sister to Alswythe, a tall and noble-looking lady, greeting her and us kindly, and so promising safe tending to her niece so long as she needed.

Here Alswythe must part from me, giving me but her hand to kiss, as also to Wulfhere, but there was a warm pressure on my hand for myself alone that bided with me. And the prioress thanked us for our care, not knowing me in the half light, and in mail, and so were we left in the courtyard, where an old lay brother, brought from the near monastery, showed us the stabling and provender for our horses, and the loft where the men should sleep, outside the walls of the inclosed building.

Here Wulfhere bade the men and boys remain, tending their horses until he should return, or until orders came from their master himself or from the lady Alswythe; for they were thralls, and not men who should be with the levy.

Then he and I went out into the roadway and walked away until we were alone.

"What now?" I asked.

"I must join my master, telling him what I have done, and that the lady is safe. So shall I march with the rest most likely. What shall I say of your part in this?"

"Nought," I answered.

"Maybe that is best--just now," he agreed.

We had come to the town streets now, and they seemed empty. The light was strong enough by this time, and there came a sound of shouting from the place of the market cross, and then we heard the bray of war horns, and Wulfhere quickened his pace, saying that the men were mustering, or maybe on the march.

Then I longed to go with him, but that might not be. So I left him at last, saying that I should surely join in the fight.

I had not gone six paces from him when he called me, and I could see that he looked anxious.

"Master," he said, "this is going to be a doubtful fight as it seems to me. Yon Danes know that the country is raised, but yet they have come back, and they mean to fight. Now our levy is raw, and has no discipline, and I doubt it will be as it was at Charnmouth. If that is so, Bridgwater will be no safe place for the lady Alswythe. She must be got hence with all speed."

"Shall you not return and hide with her?" I asked.

"That is as the master bids," said he, and then he added, looking at me doubtfully, "I would you were not so bent on this fight."

Then was I torn two ways--by my longing to strike a blow for Wessex, and by my love for my Alswythe and care for her safety. And I knew not what to say. Wulfhere understood my silence, and then decided for me.

"You have hearkened to me before, master, and now I will speak again. Get you to your place of last night on Combwich Hill, and there look on the fight; or, if it be nearer this, find such a place as you know. Then, if there is victory for us, all is well: but if not, you could not aid with your one strength to regain it. Then will Alswythe need you."

"I would fain fight," I said, still doubting.

"Aye, master; but already have you done well, and deserved well of the sheriff, and of all. He bade you fight not today--let it be so. There is loyalty also in obedience, and ever must some bide with the things one holds dear."

"I will do as you say," said I shortly, and so I turned and went.

He stood and looked after me for a little, and then he too hurried away towards the cross. Then I skirted round the town, and waited at that place where I had met with the old woman, until I saw the van of our forces marching down the road towards Cannington. These I kept up with by hurrying from point to point alongside the road, as best I might.

They were a gallant show to look on, gay with banners and bright armour. Yet I had heard of the ways of armies, and thought to see them marching in close order and in silence. But they were in a long line with many gaps, and here and there the mounted thanes rode to and fro, seemingly trying to make them close up. And they sang and shouted as they went.

When we came to the steep rise of Cannington hill, some of those thanes spurred on and rode to the summit, and there waited a little, till the men joined them. There was silence, and a closing up as they breasted the steep pitch; and then I must go through woods, and so lost sight of them for a while. I passed close to my own hall--closed and deserted. Every soul in all the countryside had fled into the town, though after the levy came a great mixed crowd of thralls and the like to see the fray.

Now here I thought to cross in the rear of the force that I might reach Combwich hill. But that was not to be.

When I saw the array again it was halted, and the men were closing up. And between the levy and that crowd of followers was a great gap, and some of these last were making for the shelter of swamp and wood. I myself was on a little rise of heathy land and could see plainly before me the road going up over the neck of

Combwich hill in the steep-sided notch there is there, where the ascent is easiest.

And that road was barred halfway up the hillside by a close-ranked company, on which the sun shone brightly, showing scarlet cloaks and gilded helms not only on the roadway, but flanking the hills on either side. These were the Danes, and behind them, over the hill, rose the smoke from Matelgar's burnt home.

Even as I looked, a great roar of defiance came from our men; but the Danes made no answer, standing still and silent. And that seemed terrible to me. So for a moment they stood, and then, as at some signal, from them broke out that deep chant with its terrible swinging melody, that had come faintly to me from Watchet haven.

Then our men rushed forward, and even where I stood I could hear the crash of arms on shields as the lines met--the ringing of the chime of war--and our men fought uphill.

And now it needed all my force to keep myself, for Alswythe's sake, from joining in that fray, and presently, when I would take my hand from my sword hilt, it was stiff and cramped from clutching hard upon it, as I watched those two lines swaying, and heard the yells of the fighters.

And indeed I should surely have joined, but there came a voice to me:

"Bide here in patience, Heregar, the king's thane! There is work for you yet that fighting will hinder."

And the old crone, Gundred, who had come I know not how, laid her hand on my arm.

"Look at the tide, Heregar, look at the tide!" she said, pointing to Parret river, where the mud banks lay bare and glistening with the falling water. "Let them drive these Danes back to their stranded ships, and how many will go home again to Denmark, think you?"

And I prayed that this might be so: for I knew she spoke truth. If they might not reach their ships, and became penned in on Stert, they were lost--every one, for none might cross the deep ooze.

"Not this time, Heregar. Remember, when the time comes," she said.

And I paid no heed to her. For now horses were galloping riderless along the road and into the fields. And men were crawling back from the fight, to fall exhausted in the rear, and then--then the steadfast line of the scarlet-cloaked Danes charged down the hill, driving our men like sheep before them.

"Up and to your work!" said the crone, pointing towards Bridgwater; and I, who had already made two steps, with drawn sword, towards that broken, flying rabble, remembered Alswythe, and turned away, groaning, to hasten to her rescue. For it was, as Wulfhere had said, all that I could do.

Swiftly I went, turning neither to right nor left along the road, hearing always behind me the cries of those who fled, and the savage shouts of the pursuing vikings. I was in the midst of that crowd of thralls once, but they thinned, taking to the woods whence I had come; while I kept on.

Then I saw one of those horses, a great white steed, standing, snorting, by the wayside where he had stopped, and I spoke to him, and he let me catch and mount him, and so I rode on.

Yet when I came to the top of Cannington Hill I looked back. All the road was full of our men, flying; and a thought came into my head, and I dared to draw rein and wait for them, linking my mail again across my face.

They came up, panting, and wild with panic, and there with voice and hand I bade them stand on that vantage ground and block the way against the Danes; bidding them remember the helpless ones in the town, who must have time to fly, and how the Danes must needs shrink from a second fight after hot pursuit.

And there is that in a Saxon's stubborn heart which bade them heed me, and there they formed up again, wild with rage and desperate, and the line grew thicker and firmer as more came up, with the sheriff himself, till the foremost pursuing Danes recoiled, and some were slain, and I knew that the flight was over.

Then I slipped from my horse and made my way on foot, lest men should notice my going, but the horse followed me, and soon I mounted him again and galloped on.

Then I found that though I had not noticed it, my mail had fallen apart: but I knew not if any had known me, or even had noted who I might be.

So I came to Bridgwater, bringing terror with me, as men gathered what had befallen from my haste. Yet I stayed for none; but went on to the nunnery.

CHAPTER IX. IN BRIDGWATER.

Two of Wulfhere's men were by the gate, lounging against the sunny wall; but they roused into life as they heard the clatter of my horse's hoofs, and came to meet me and take the bridle, as was their duty. They knew who I was well enough; but thralls may not question the ways of a thane, as I was yet in their eyes, though outlawed. Yet they asked me for news of the fight, and I told them--lest they should raise a panic, or maybe leave us themselves--only that our men stood against the Danes on Cannington Hill, and that beyond them the invaders could not come. And that satisfied them.

I was doubtful whether to go in at once and seek audience with the prioress, or wait until some fresh news came in; for now I began to have a hope that our men would sweep down the hill on the Danes and scatter them in turn, even as they had themselves been overborne. So for half an hour I waited, pacing the road before the nunnery, while I bade the men see to my horse; but the place was very quiet, being on that side the town away from the fight, so that any coming thence would stay their flight when the shelter of the houses was reached.

At last came one, running at a steady pace, and I sprang to meet him, for it was Wulfhere. His face was hard and set, his armour was covered with blood, and he had a bandage round his head instead of helmet; but he was not hurt much, as one might see by the way he came.

He grasped my hand without a word, and threw himself on the bank by the road side to get breath, and I stood by him, silent for a while.

"Heregar," he said at last, "it is well for Bridgwater town, and these here in this nunnery, that you obeyed and fought not."

"Wherefore?" I said. "Must we fly?"

"I saw you rally the men on Cannington Hill, and that was the best thing done in all this evil day."

"Then," I asked, "do they yet stand?"

"Aye; for the Danes have drawn off, and our men bar the way here."

I told him what I had hoped from a charge of our levy; but he shook his head and told me that, even had our men the skill to see their advantage, the Danes had formed up again on seeing that this might be, and had gone back in good order to their first post at Combwich.

"But our levy will not bide a second fight," he said sadly. "Already the men are making off home, in twos and threes, saying that the Danes will depart, and the like. Tomorrow the way here will be open, for there will be no force left to Osric by the morning. I have seen such things before."

"Then must the Lady Alswythe fly," I said: "but where is Matelgar?"

"Struck down as he fled," said Wulfhere grimly. "I saw Osric and twenty of his men close round him and beat back the Danes for a moment: but I could not win to them, and so came back to you as you rallied us. That was well done," he said again.

"I left when Osric came up. Matelgar I saw not," I said.

"Osric saw you, though," answered Wulfhere, "and, moreover, knew you. And I heard him cry out when he saw the white horse riderless; for the arrows were still flying, and he thought you slain, I think."

Now I wondered if Osric would be wroth with me, thinking I had fought against his orders; but I had little time to think of myself, all my care being for Alswythe, who had lost home and father in one day; being left to Wulfhere, and me--an outlaw.

Then Wulfhere and I took counsel about flight, being troubled also about the holy women in this place; for the heathen would not respect the walls of a nunnery. But for them we thought Osric would surely care.

Now there came to us as we stood and talked, a housecarle in a green cloak, and asked us if we had seen a warrior, wounded maybe, riding a great white horse, which, he added, had been Edred the Thane's, who was killed.

"Aye, that have I," said Wulfhere, "what of him?"

"Osric the Sheriff seeks him. Tell me quickly where I may find him."

"Is Osric back in the town?" asked Wulfhere in surprise.

"Aye, man, and half the levy with him. The Danes will go away now. Enough are left to mind them."

Then Wulfhere stamped on the ground in rage, cursing the folly of every man of the levy. And the housecarle stared at him as at one gone suddenly mad; but I knew only too well that his worst fears were on the way to be realized, and that soon there would be no force left on Cannington Hill.

Suddenly he turned on the messenger and asked if he knew the name of the man he sought.

"No; but men say that it was one Heregar--an outlawed thane. And some say that it was one of the saints."

"Will Osric string him up, think you, if he can catch him, and it be Heregar only, and no saint?"

The man stared again.

"Surely not," he said, "for he was sore cast down once, on the hill, thinking him slain. But men had seen him remount and ride on, And Osric bid me, and all of us who seek him, pray Heregar--if Heregar it be-- to come to him in all honour. Let me go and seek him."

Then Wulfhere turned to me and asked if I would go. And at that the man made reverence to me, giving his message again.

Then I said "Is Matelgar the Thane with him?" and he answered that Matelgar was slain before the stand was made.

Then I said I would go, if only to ask Osric for a guard to keep the Lady Alswythe safe in her flight. And Wulfhere agreed, but doubtfully, saying that nevertheless he would make ready the horses and provisions for a journey, biding till I came back, or sent a messenger.

So I went with the housecarle, who led me again through the marketplace to that same great house whence I had been sent forth overnight. All the square was full of men, drinking deeply, some boasting of their deeds, and some of deeds to be done yet. But many sat silent and gloomy, and more cried out with pain as their wounds were dressed by the leeches or the womenfolk. All was confusion, and, indeed, one might not know if this turmoil was after victory or defeat.

None noticed me or my guide, but, indeed, I saw few men I knew in all the crowd, for the men of Bridgwater and those of Matelgar's following had fought most fiercely on their own land, and even now stayed to guard what they might on the hill.

Osric again sat in the great chair in the hall, as I could see through the open door, and round him were the thanes; but far fewer than last night. And presently a housecarle spoke to him, and he rose up and left the hall. Then they led me to a smaller chamber, and there he was alone, and waiting for me.

Now I knew not what his wish to see me might mean, but from him I looked for no harm, remembering how he had seemed to favour me even in refusing my request. But, least of all did I look for him to come forward to meet me, taking both my hands, and grasping them, while he thanked me for the day's work.

"Lightly I let you go last night, Heregar," he said, "setting little store on the matter among all the trouble of the gathering. But when I sent you away and forgot you, surely the saints guided me. For I have heard how you dared to go down to Stert and warn us all, and I saw you stay the flight, even now. Much praise, and more than that, is due to you. Were you in the fight?"

Then I could answer him to a plain question; for all this praise, though it was good to hear, abashed me.

"Nay, Sheriff," I answered. "Fain would I have been there, but a wiser head than mine advised me, and bade me do your bidding, and forbear. Else should I surely have fought."

"Loyalty has brought good to us all, Heregar," he said, looking squarely at me. "Yet should I have hardly blamed you had you disobeyed me."

Then I flushed red, thinking shame not to have done so, and went to excuse myself for obedience.

"Yet had I the safety of a lady who must die, if the battle went wrongly for us, laid on me in a way," I said.

"Matelgar's fair daughter?" he asked.

"Aye, Sheriff," And I told him of the flight from the hall, and where she was now, wondering how he guessed this. But I had come from Stert, and therefore the guess was no wonder. He looked at me gravely, and then sat down, motioning me to be seated also. He treated me not as an outlaw, I thought.

"Matelgar is dead," he said. "I saw him fall, and tried to bring him off. He was not yet sped when we beat off the Danes. And he had time to speak to me."

I bowed in silence, not knowing what to say. Strange that, now my enemy was dead, I had no joy in it; but I thought of Alswythe only.

The sheriff went on, looking at me closely.

"He bade me find Heregar, the outlawed thane who spoke last night to me, and bid him forgive. Then he died, and I must needs leave him, for the Danes came on in force."

Still I was silent, for many thoughts came up in my heart and choked me. How I had hated him, and yet how he had wronged me--even to seeking my life. Yet was I beginning to think of him but as a bad father to my Alswythe, but a man to be held in some regard, for the sake of her love to him. And it seems to me that shaping my words to this end so often had gradually turned my utter bitterness away: for one has to make one's thoughts go the way one speaks, if one would seem to speak true.

"I may not make out all this, Heregar, my friend," said the sheriff; "but that you were disloyal ever, no man may say in my hearing after this day's work. And I know that Matelgar was the foremost in accusing you. Wherefore it seems to me that there was work there to be forgiven by you. Is that so?"

The thing was so plain that I could but bow my head in assent.

"Now," he went on, "I have heard private talk of this sort before now; but never mind. I cannot inlaw you again, Heregar; for that must needs be done in full Moot, as was the outlawry. Yet shall all my power be bent to help you back to your own, if only for the sake of today."

Then would I thank him, but he stopped me.

"To the man who lit the fire of Stert, who checked the panic on Cannington Hill, thanks are due, not gratitude from him. And to him justice and reward."

Now I knew not what to say; but at that moment came a hurried rapping on the door and the sound of voices, speaking together. Then the door was thrown open and a man entered, heated and breathless, crying:

"The Danes--they are on our men again!"

Then Osric flushed red, and his eyes sparkled, and he bid the thanes who crowded after the messenger get to horse and sound the assembly at once to go to the assistance of those who were yet on the hill.

And yet he turned to me when this was said, and took my hand again.

"Get your lady in safety to Glastonbury, where Ealhstan the Bishop is. I will care for the nuns if need be. Take this ring of mine and show it to him, and then ride with it to Eanulf the Ealdorman and tell him of our straits. The words I leave to you, who have done better than all of us today."

Then he took helm and sword from one who brought them in haste, and armed himself, while I, putting the ring he had given me on my finger, yet stood beside him. When he was armed he turned sharply to me.

"You want to fight again," he said. "Well, I will not blame you; but believe me, you will do more for us in going to Eanulf than in spending your life here for nought."

Then he saw he had said too much, perhaps, and motioning his man out of the room, so that we were alone, he went on quickly: "I say for nought, because all I can do is to hold back the Danes for a little; you have seen how it is. We are evenly matched in numbers, or thereabout; but they are trained and hardened warriors, and our poor men are all unused to war. Moreover, Heregar, these Danes come to fight, and our men do but fight because they must. Now I will send one after you to Glastonbury to let you know how this matter goes; but it will be, I fear, no pleasant message."

Then would I not ask him for men as I had been minded to do, knowing what a strait he was in, and that his words were only too true. Those two differences between Dane and Saxon in those days of the first fighting left the victory too plainly on the side of the newcomers. And they sum up all the reasons for the headway they made against us till Alfred, our wise king, taught us to meet them in their own way.

So once more I felt the grip of Osric's hand on mine, and I left him, with a heavy heart indeed, but with a new hope for myself and for Alswythe, in the end.

I stood for a moment before I turned out of the marketplace, eating a loaf I had taken from the table as I passed, and watching the men gather, spiritless, for this new fight. On many, too, the strong ale had told, and it was a sorry force that Osric could take with him.

But I might not stay, and was turning to go, when I saw one standing like myself and watching, close by. It was my host of Sedgemoor, Dudda the Collier. And never was face more welcome than his grimy countenance, for now I knew that I had found one who, in an hour, would take Alswythe into paths where none might follow, and that, too, on the nearest road to Glastonbury. There is no safer place for those who would fly, than the wastes of Sedgemoor to those who know, or have guide to them, and there no Danes would ever come.

So I stepped up to him and touched him, and he grinned at seeing a known face, muttering to himself, "Grendel, the king's messenger."

And as I beckoned he willingly followed me towards my destination, asking me of the fight, and what was on hand now so suddenly.

I told him shortly, finding that he had been drawn from his own neighbourhood by curiosity, which must be satisfied before he went back. And I told him that now the Danes were close on Bridgwater, and that I must bear messages to Eanulf the Ealdorman. Would he earn a good reward by getting me and some others across Sedgemoor by the paths along which he had led me?

And at that he grinned, delighted, saying, "Aye, that will I, master," seeming to forget all else in prospect of gain.

So I bade him follow me closely, and soon we were back at the nunnery gates.

They were open, and inside I could see the horses standing. Wulfhere was waiting for me, looking anxious; but his brow cleared as he saw me, and he asked for the news, saying that he feared I had fallen into the wrong hands.

Then I told him I had, as I thought, no more to fear, showing him the sheriff's ring and telling him of my errand.

"That is nigh as good as inlawed again," he said gladly. "Anyway, you ride as the sheriff's man now."

Then his face clouded a little, and he added, "But Glastonbury is a far cry, master, for the roads are none so direct."

Then I called the collier, and Wulfhere questioned him, and soon was glad as I that I had met with him, saying that in an hour we should be in safety. But he would that the prioress and her ladies would come also, for he knew that Osric's fears would be only too true. Then must we go and tell Alswythe of the journey she must make; and how to tell of her father's death I knew not, nor did Wulfhere. And there we two men were helpless, looking at one another in the courtyard, and burning with impatience to get off.

"Let us go first, and tell her on the way" said he.

But I reminded him that we were here even now, and not on the far side of the Quantocks, because she would by no means leave her father.

Now while we debated this, the old sister who was portress, opened the wicket and asked us through it why these horses stood in the yard, and what we armed men did there. And that decided me. I would ask for speech with the prioress, and tell her the trouble.

That pleased Wulfhere: and I did so. Then the portress asked who I might be, and lest my name should but prove a bar to speech with the lady, I showed her Osric's ring, which she knew as one he was wont to give to men as surety that they came from him on his errand. And that was enough, for in a few minutes she came back, taking me to the guest chamber.

There I unhelmed and waited, while those minutes seemed very long, though they were but few before the lady came in.

She started a little when she saw who I was, for she had known me well, and knew now in what case I had been. But Alswythe had told her also of what I had been able to do for her last night, if she had heard no more, for news gets inside even closed walls, in one way or another, from the lay people who serve the place.

I bent my knee to her, and she looked at me very sadly, saying: "I knew and loved your mother, Heregar, my son, and sorely have I grieved for you--not believing all the things brought against you. How come you here now?"

Then I held out my hand and showed her Osric's ring, only saying that as the good sheriff trusted me I would ask her to do so. And at that she looked glad, and said that she would hold Osric's trust as against any word she had heard of me in dispraise.

So I bowed, and then, thinking it foolish to waste time, begged her to forgive bluntness, and told her of the death of Matelgar and of the sore danger of the town, and of how Osric had bidden me take Alswythe to Glastonbury to the bishop, and how he would himself care for her own safety.

She was a brave lady, and worthy of the race of Offa from which she sprung. And she heard me to the end, only growing very pale, while her hand that rested on the table grew yet whiter as she clenched it.

"Can we not recover the body of the thane?" she asked, speaking very low.

I could but shake my head, for I knew that where he lay was now in the hands of the Danes. True, if Osric could beat them off again he might gain truce for such recovery on both sides; but that seemed hopeless to me. Then I was bold to add:

"Now, lady, this matter is pressing, and in your hands I must leave it. Trust the Lady Alswythe to me and her faithful servant, Wulfhere, and I will be answerable for her with my life. But of her father's death I dare not tell her."

Then she bowed her head a little, and, I think, was praying. For when she looked at me again her face was very calm though so pale.

"Alswythe has told me of you, Heregar, my son," she said, "and to you will I trust her. Moreover I will bid her go at once, and I will tell her that heavy news you bring. You will not have long to wait, for in truth we are ready, fearing such as this."

Then I kissed her hand, and she blessed me, and went from the room. And, taught by her example, I prayed that I might not fail in this trust, but find safety for her I loved.

Now came the sister who had charge of such things, and set before me a good meal with wine, saying no word, but signing the cross over all in token that I might eat, and glad enough was I to do so, though in haste. Yet before I would begin I asked that sister to let Wulfhere know that all was going right, and to bid him be ready. She said no word, as must have been their rule, but went out, and I knew afterwards that she sent one to tell him.

In a quarter hour or so, and when I, refreshed with the good food I so needed, was waxing restless and impatient, the prioress came back, and signed me to follow her, and taking my helm, I did so, till we came to the great door leading to the courtyard. There stood Alswythe, very pale, and trying to stop her weeping very bravely, and she gave me her hand for a moment, without a word, and it was cold as ice, and shook a little; yet it had a lingering grasp on mine, as though it would fain rest with me for a little help.

There were but two of her maidens with her, and the prioress saw that I was surprised, and said: "The rest bide with us, Heregar, and here they will surely be safe. Alswythe will take no more than these, lest you are hindered on the journey."

And I was glad of that, though I should have loved to see her better attended, as befitted her; yet need was pressing, and this was best. Then the prioress kissed Alswythe and the maidens, and Wulfhere set them on their horses, for though I would fain help Alswythe myself, the lady had more to say to me, and kept me.

She told me to take my charge to the abbess of her own order at Glastonbury, where they would be tended in all honour as here with herself, and she gave me a letter also to the abbess to tell her what was needed and why they came, and then she gave me a bag with gold in it, knowing that I might have to buy help on the way. For all this I thanked her; but she said that rather it was I who should be thanked, and from henceforward, if her word should in any way have weight, it should go with that of Osric the Sheriff for my welfare.

And this seemed to me to be much said before my task was done, but afterwards I knew that she had talked with Wulfhere, who had told her all--even to the treachery of Matelgar. That would I have prevented, had I known, but so it was to be, and I had no knowledge of it till long after. Wulfhere had been called in to give her news while I was with Osric, yet he had not dared to tell her of the thane's death.

All being ready, I mounted that white steed that had been the dead thane's, knowing that in war and haste these things must be taken as they come, and that he was better in Saxon hands than Danish. Then I gave the word, and we started, Dudda the Collier going by my side, and staring at the prioress and all things round him.

Alswythe turned and looked hard at her aunt as we passed the gates, and I also. She stood very still on the steps before the great door, with the portress beside her. There was only the old lay brother in the court beside, and so we left her. And what my fears were for her and hers I could not tell Alswythe. For, as we left the gates, something in the sky over towards the battleground caught my eyes, and I turned cold with dread. It was the smoke from burning houses at Cannington.

CHAPTER X. FLIGHT THROUGH SEDGEMOOR.

I was glad we had not to go through the town, for the sights there were such as Alswythe could not bear to look on. And if that smoke meant aught, it meant that our men were beaten back, and would even now be flying into the place with perhaps the Danes at their heels.

I rode alongside Wulfhere, and motioned to him to look, and as he did so he groaned. Then he spoke quite cheerfully to his lady, saying that we had better push on and make a good start; and so we broke into a steady trot and covered the ground rapidly enough, ever away from danger.

I rode next Alswythe, but I would not dare speak to her as yet. She had her veil down, and was quite silent, and I felt that it would be best for me to wait for her wish.

Beside me trotted the collier, Wulfhere was leading, and next to Alswythe and me came the two maidens. After them came the three men and two boys, all mounted, and leading with them the other three horses of the twelve we had brought from Stert. They were laden with things for the journey given by the prioress, and with what they had saved from Matelgar's hall, though that was little enough.

Wulfhere would fain have made the collier ride one of these spare horses; but the strange man had refused, saying that his own legs he could trust, but not those of a four-footed beast.

It was seven in the bright May morning when Dane and Saxon met on Combwich Hill. It was midday when I met Wulfhere at the nunnery, and now it was three hours and more past. But I thought there was yet light enough left for us to find our way across Sedgemoor, and lodge that night in safety in the village near the collier's hut; and so, too, thought Wulfhere when I, thinking that perhaps Alswythe's grief might find its own solace in tears when I was not by her, rode on beside him for a while.

"Once set me on Polden hills, master," said Wulfhere, "I can do well enough, knowing that country from my youth. But this is a good chance that has sent you your friend the collier."

So he spoke, and then I fell to wondering, if it was all chance, as we say, that led my feet in that night of wandering to Dudda's hut, that now I might find help in sorer need than that. For few there are who could serve as guide over that waste of fen and swamp, and but for him we must needs have kept the main roads, far longer in their way to Glastonbury, as skirting Sedgemoor, and now to be choked with flying people.

Presently Wulfhere asked me if in that village we might find one good house where to lodge the Lady Alswythe. And I told him that there I had not been, but at least knew of one substantial franklin, for my playfellow, Turkil, had been the son of such an one, as I was told. The collier, who ran, holding my stirrup leather, tireless on his lean limbs as a deerhound, heard this, and told me that the man's house was good and strong--not like those in Bridgwater--but a great house for these parts. So I was satisfied enough.

Then this man Dudda, finding I listened to him in that matter, began to talk, asking me questions of the fighting, and presently "if I had seen the saint?"

I asked him what he meant; and as I did so I heard Wulfhere chuckle to himself. Then he told me a wild story that was going round the town. How that, when all seemed lost, there came suddenly a wondrous vision, rising up before the men, of a saint clad in armour and riding a white horse, having his face covered lest men should be blinded by the light thereof, who, standing with drawn sword on Cannington Hill, so bade the men take courage that they turned and beat the Danes back. Whereupon he vanished, though the white horse yet remained for a little, before it, too, was gone.

Well, thought I, Grendel the fiend was I but the other day, and now I am to be a saint. And with that I could not restrain myself, but laughed as once before I had laughed at this same man, for the very foolishness of the thing. Yet I might not let Alswythe know that I laughed, and so could not let it go as I would, and I saw that Wulfhere was laughing likewise, silently.

Now this is not to be wondered at, though it was but a little thing maybe. For we had been like a long-bent bow, overstrained with doubt and anxiety, and, now that we were in safety with the lady, it needed but like this to slacken the tension, and bid our minds relieve themselves. So that laugh did us both good, and moreover took away some of the downcast look from our faces when next we spoke to our charge.

When he could speak again, Wulfhere answered the man, still smiling.

"Aye, man, I saw him. And he was wondrous like Heregar, our master, here."

And at that the collier stared at me, and then said: "There be painted saints in our church. But they be not like mortal men, being no wise so well-favoured as the master."

And that set Wulfhere laughing again, for the good monks who paint these things are seldom good limners, but make up for bad drawing by bright colour. So that one may only know saint from fiend by the gold, or the want of it, round his head.

Then fell I to thinking again about myself, and what it takes to make man a saint or a fiend. And that thought was a long thought.

Now were we come across Parret, and began our journey into the fens. And presently we must ride in single file along a narrow pathway which I could barely trace, and indeed in places could not make out at all. And here the collier led, going warily, then came Wulfhere, and then Alswythe, with myself next behind her to help if need were. After us the maidens, and then the rest.

So we were in safety, for half a mile of this ground was safer than a wall behind us. We went silently for a little while, save for a few words of caution here and there. But at last Alswythe turned to me, and lifted her veil, smiling a little to me at last, and asking why we left the good roads for this wild place, for though we men were used to the like in hunting, she knew not that such places and paths could be, brought up as she was in the wooded uplands of our own corner of the country.

I told her how I was to make all speed to Glastonbury, and that this was the nearest road: and she was content, being very trustful in both her protectors. But then she asked if that place should be reached before dark, having little knowledge of places or distances.

Then I must needs tell how we were bound for that village where the hermit was, and Turkil of whom I had told her, seeing that it was over late to reach the town, but that there we hoped to come next day. And she said she would fain see those two, "and maybe Grendel also," smiling again a little to please me. And I knew how much that little jest cost her to make, and loved her the more for her thought for me. Then she was silent for a while.

Presently one of the men in the rear shouted, and there was a great splashing and snorting of horses, and we looked round. One of the led horses had gone off the path and was in a bog, and that had set the rest rearing with fright.

So we had to halt, and Wulfhere gave his horse to Dudda to hold while he went back. And that kept us for a while waiting, and then I could stand beside Alswythe for a little.

"I have seen the last of my outlaw, they tell me," she said, wanting to learn how things were with me.

Yet I was still that, if only for loss of lands and place. Though as Osric's chosen messenger I had that last again for a little, because of his need.

So I told her that that matter must be settled by the Moot, but that Osric was my friend, and that while I bore his ring at least none might call me "outlaw". And at that she was glad, and told me that if she saw Leofwine the hermit she would tell him that his words were coming true. Then she looked hard at me, and said that she had heard from her aunt why Osric so trusted me, and that she was proud of Heregar. And I said that I had but done the things that someone had to do, and which came in my way, as it seemed to me, wherein I was fortunate.

At that she smiled at me, seeming to think more of the matter than that, and so talked of other things. Yet she must needs at last come to that which lay nearest her heart, and so asked me if I had seen her father fall.

And I was glad to say that I had not; adding that it was near Combwich Hill, as I had heard, and close to where Osric the Sheriff fought.

So I think that all her life long she believed him to have fallen fighting in the first line, where Osric was, with his face to the enemy; for all men spoke well of the sheriff's valour that day, and none would say more than I told her. Yet it may have been that the thane fought well, unobserved, in that press, and there is perhaps little blame to many who fly in a panic.

Now, that spoken of and passed over, she became more like her brave self, and from that time on would speak cheerfully both to Wulfhere and myself, as, the horses set in order again, we once more went on our winding way, following our guide.

Glad was I when, just before sunset, we saw the woodland under which his hut was set, and heard the vesper bell ringing far off from the village church. Soon we were on hard ground again, and then I could show Alswythe where I had played Grendel unwittingly, and point the way I had wandered from Brent.

There we rested the horses, for we had yet two miles to go, and they were weary with the long and heavy travelling of the fens. And Alswythe would go into the hut, and there her maidens brought her food and wine, and we stayed for half an hour.

Wulfhere and I looked out towards Bridgwater town, now seeming under the very hills, in the last sunlight. Smoke rose from behind it, but that was doubtless from Cannington; yet there were other clouds of smoke rising against the sun, and as he looked at these the old warrior said that he feared the worst, for surely the

Danes were spreading over the country and that need for them to keep together was gone.

"If we see not Bridgwater on fire by tomorrow," he said, "it will be a wonder."

But we knew that we could bide here for this night safe as if no Danes were nearer than the Scaw.

After that rest we rode on through the woodland path, down which they had come to exorcise me, till we saw before us in the gray twilight the church and houses of the village, pleasant with light from door and window, and noise of barking dogs, as we crossed the open mark [viii].

Dudda the Collier led us to the largest house which stood on the little central green round which the buildings clustered, and there the door stood open, and a tall man with a small boy beside him looked out to see what was disturbing the dogs. Behind them the firelight shone red on a pleasant and large room where we could see men at supper.

And the light shone out on me, for the boy sprang out from his father's side, shouting that it was "Grendel come back again", and running to me to greet me.

So we found a welcome in that quiet place, and soon the good franklin's wife came out, bustling and pitiful in her care for Alswythe and sorrow for her need to fly from her lost home, for it took but few words to explain what had befallen.

They brought us in, and the thralls left supper to tend our horses, though Wulfhere would go with them to see that done before he joined us in the wide oak-built room that made all the lower floor of the house. Overhead was the place where Alswythe and her maidens should be, and built against the walls outside were the thralls' quarters, save for a few who slept in the lower room round the great fire.

Now, how they treated us it needs not to be told, for it was in the way of a good Somerset franklin, and that is saying much. But that night he would talk little, seeing that I and Wulfhere were overdone with want of sleep. Indeed it was but the need of caution that had kept me from falling asleep on my horse more than once on the road. So very soon they brought us skins and cloaks, and we stretched ourselves before the fire, and warmed, and cleansed, and well refreshed with food and drink, fell to sleep on the instant.

Yet not so soundly could I sleep at first, but that I woke once, thinking I heard the yells of the Danes close on us: but it was some farmyard sound from without, and peaceful.

Then I slept again until, towards dawning I think, I awoke, shivering, and with a great untellable fear on me, and saw a tall, gray figure standing by my couch. And I looked, and lo it was Matelgar the Thane.

Then I went to rouse Wulfhere, but my hand would not be stretched out, and the other men slept heavily, so that I lay still and looked in the dead thane's face and grew calmer.

For his face was set with a look of sorrow such as I had never seen there, and he gazed steadfastly at me and I at him, and the grief in his face did but deepen. And at last he spoke, and the voice was his own, and yet not his own.

"Heregar, sorely have I wronged you," he said, "and my rest is troubled therefor. Yet, when I heard what you had done for mine last night, my heart was sore within me, and I repented of all, and would surely have made amends. And now it is too late, and my body lies dishonoured on Parret side while I am here. Yet do you forgive, and mayhap I shall rest."

Then I strove to speak, bidding him know that I forgave, but I could not, and he seemed to grow more sad, watching me yet. And when I saw that, I made a great effort, and stretching my hand towards him signed the blessed sign in token that that should bid me forgive him, so leaving my hand outstretched towards him.

And then his face changed and grew brighter, and he took my hand in his, as I might see, though I could feel nought but a chill pass on it, as it were, and spoke again, saying:

"It is well, and shall be, both with you and me. And when you need me I shall stand by you once again and make amends."

Then he was gone, and my hand fell from where his had been, and straightway I slept again in a dreamless sleep till Wulfhere roused me in the full morning light.

And in that light this matter seemed to me but a dream that had come to me. Yet even as I should have wished to speak to Alswythe's father, had I done, and I would not have had it otherwise. Then the dream in a way comforted me, being good to think on, for I would not willingly be at enmity with any man, or living or dead. But that it was only a dream seemed more sure, because in it Matelgar had said he knew of my saving Alswythe. And Wulfhere and I had agreed not to tell him that. Also I had little need of Matelgar living, in good truth, and surely less need of him now that he was gone past making amends.

Down into the great chamber to break her fast with us came Alswythe, bright and fresh, and with her grief put on one side, for our sakes who served her. And Turkil talked gaily with both Alswythe and me and Wulfhere, and would fain tell all the story of how he sought the fire-spitting fiend and was disappointed.

Then I missed the collier, and asked where he was. He had gone to bring the good hermit the franklin told me, and would be back shortly.

Now, when we had broken our fast it was yet very early, and the villagers must needs hear all the news of the great fight and terror beyond the fens, and as they heard, a growl of wrath went round, and the men grasped spade and staff and fork fiercely, bidding the franklin lead them at once to join the levy.

But Wulfhere told them that they needs must now wait a second raising, and that I was even now on my way to Eanulf the Ealdorman to tell him of the need. Then the franklin asked that he and his might go with me, but I, seeing that for an outlaw to take a following with him was not to be thought of, bade them wait for word and sure tidings of the gathering place.

While we talked thus the little bell in the church turret began to ring, and we knew that the hermit, Leofwine the priest, had come, and would say mass for us. Then, perhaps, was such a gathering to pray for relief for their land, as had not been since those days, far off now, when the British prayed, in that same place, the like prayers for deliverance from my own forbears. And as I prayed, looking on the calm face of the old man who had bidden me take heart and forgive, I knew that last night's dream was true in this, that I had forgiven.

So when the mass was over, and Wulfhere had begged Alswythe to take order at once for our going on our journey, I found the old man, and could greet him with a light heart. And he, looking on me, could read, as he had read the trouble, how that that had passed, and asked me if all was well, as my face seemed to say.

I told him how I had fared, and how my outlawry, though still in force, was now light on me as the sheriff's messenger--though this I thought was but because, flying with Alswythe, I might as well take the message as one who could be less easily spared.

Then he said that already he deemed the prophecy that had been given him was coming true, and spoke many good and loving words to me to strengthen my thoughts of peace withal.

Presently he looked at our horses, now standing ready at the franklin's door, and would have me go back with him into his own chamber in the little timber-walled church. And there he found writing things in a chest, and wrote on a slip of parchment a letter which he bade me give to the bishop when I came to him, signing it with his name at the end, as he told me, though I could not read it, for one who has been bred a hunter and warrior has no need for the arts of the clerk. Indeed, I had seen but two men write before, and one was our old priest at Cannington, and the other was Matelgar, and I ever wondered that this latter should be able to do so, and why of late he was often sending men with letters. Yet it seems to me now that surely they had to do with his schemes that had so come to nought.

Then the old man blessed me, telling me again that I should surely prosper unless that I failed by my own fault, and that it seemed to him that there was yet work for me to do that should set me again in my place, and maybe higher.

So talking with him, Wulfhere called me, and I must needs say farewell to Turkil and his father, and they bade us return, when the time came, by this way back to our own place. And Turkil wept, and would fain have gone with us, but I promised to see him again, and waved hand to him before the broad meadows of the mark were passed, and the woods hid the village from us.

Then did Alswythe, in her kindness, fall into a like mistake as that I had made with the boy; for she turned to me, smiling, and said that she would surely take him into her service at Stert, and see to his training hereafter, but then remembered that she had no longer home, and her smile faded into tears.

My heart ached for her, knowing I could give her no comfort. After that we rode in silence, and quickly, for the track was good.

Now there is little to tell of that ride till we reached the hilltop that Wulfhere knew, and where we could look down on the land we were to cross, and fancy we could see Glastonbury far away. Here Dudda the Collier's task was ended, and I called him to me, pulling out the purse the good prioress had given me, that I might give him a gold piece for his faithful service.

He stood before me, cap in hand, and I gave him a bright new coin, and he took it, turning it over curiously.

"Take it, Dudda," I said, "you have earned it well."

Then he grinned in his way, and answered: "It is no good to me, master. I pray you give me silver instead. Like were I to starve if life lay in the changing of this among our poor folk."

So I turned over the money to find silver, but there was not enough, and so I took out that bag which I had found in the roadway, and had not opened since, having almost forgotten it. There was silver and copper only in that, and I began to give him his reward.

But still the man hesitated, and seemed anxious to ask me something, and, while I counted out the money, he spoke: "Master, the men call you Heregar, and that is an outlaw's name."

"Well." said I, fearing no reproach from that just now, and being sure that by this time the man knew all about me from our thralls with us. "Heregar, the outlawed thane I was, and am, except that the sheriff has bid me ride on his business."

"Then, master," said he, "give me no reward but to serve you. No man's man am I, either free or unfree, but son of escaped thralls who are dead long ago. Therefore am I outlaw also by all rights, and would fain follow you. And it seems to me that you will need one to mind your steed."

Now this was a long speech for the collier, who, as I had learnt, could hold his tongue: and we were short-handed also, with all these horses. Therefore I told him that it should be as he would, for service offered freely in this way was like to be faithful, seeing that there had been trial on both sides. But I gave him four silver pennies, which he would have refused, but that I bade him think of them as fasten pennies, which contented him well.

This, too, pleased both Alswythe and Wulfhere, who were glad of the addition to our party. So we rode on. But many were the far-off columns of smoke we looked back on beyond Parret, before the hills rose behind us and hid them.

CHAPTER XI. EALHSTAN THE BISHOP.

It was in the late afternoon when we rode into Glastonbury town, past the palisadings of the outer works, and then among cottages, and here and there a timber house of the better sort, till we came to the great abbey. It was not so great then as now, nor is it now as it will be, for ever have pious hands built so that those who come after may have room to add if they will. But it was the greatest building that I had ever seen, and, moreover, of stone throughout, which seemed wonderful to me. And there, too, Wulfhere showed me the thorn tree which sprang from the staff of the blessed Joseph of Arimathea, which flowers on Christmas Day, ever.

Then we came to the nunnery where we should leave Alswythe, and I, for my part, was sorry that the journey was over, sad though it had been in many ways, for when I must leave her I knew not how long it should be, if ever, before I saw her again.

And I think the same thought was in her heart, for, when Wulfhere showed her the great house, she sighed, looking at me a little, and I could say nothing. But she began to thank us two for our care of her, as though we could have borne to take less than we had. And her words were so sweet and gracious that even the old warrior could not find wherewith to answer her, and we both bowed our heads in thanks, and rode, one on each side of her, in silence.

Then she must ask Wulfhere what he would do when she was safely bestowed. And that was a plain question he could answer well.

"Truly, lady, if you will give me leave, I would see Heregar, our master, through whatever comes of his messages."

Then was I very glad, and the more that, though I might not think myself such, the old warrior would call me his master, for that told me that he had full belief in me.

Yet I could but say: "Friend should you call me, Wulfhere, my good counsellor, not master."

And I reached out my hand to him, bowing to Alswythe, whose horse's neck I must cross. And Wulfhere took it, and on our two rough hands Alswythe laid her white fingers, pressing them, and, looking from one to the other, said:

"Two such friends I think no woman ever had, or wiser, or braver. Go on together as you will, and yet forget not me here in Glastonbury."

Then we loosed our hands, looking, maybe, a little askance, for our Saxon nature will oft be ashamed, if one may call it so, of a good impulse acted on, and Wulfhere said that we must think of those things hereafter.

When we came to the gate there was a little crowd following us, for word had gone round in some way that we were fugitives from Parret side. But Wulfhere had bade the men answer no questions till we had seen the bishop, lest false reports should go about the place. So the crowd melted away soon, and we knocked, asking admission, and showing the letter from the prioress of Bridgwater.

Now here there was much state, as it seemed, and we must wait for a little, but then the gates were thrown open, and we rode through them into the courtyard, which was large and open. Then opened a great door on the left, and there was the abbess with many sisters, and one asked me for the letter we bore. So I gave it, and, standing there, the abbess read it while we waited.

As she read she grew pale, and then flushed again, and at last, after twice reading, came down the steps, all her state forgotten, and with tears embraced Alswythe, giving thanks for her safety. And then, leaving her, she came to me where I sat, unhelmed, and gave me her hand, thanking me for all I had done, and, as she said, perhaps for the safety of the Bridgwater sisters also.

Then all of a sudden she went back up the steps, where the sisters were whispering together, and became cold and stately again, so that I wondered if I had offended her in not speaking, which I dared not.

When she was back again in her place, she bade Alswythe and her maidens welcome, and added that all her sister prioress asked her she would do. Also, that one would come and show us lodging for men and horses, which should be at the expense of the nunnery.

So Alswythe must needs part from us coldly, even as she had joined us at Bridgwater, as a noble lady from her attendants, giving us her hand to kiss only. But I went back to my horse well content, knowing that her love and thoughts went out to me.

She went through the great door, but it closed not so fast but that I might see the abbess put her arm around her very tenderly, her state forgotten again, and I knew that she was in good hands.

Now when the horses were stabled, and our men knew where they should bide in the strangers' lodgings--set apart for the trains of guests to the nunnery, which were very spacious--Wulfhere and I must needs find the way to get audience of the bishop. As far as the doors of the abbey where he abode was easy enough, but there, waiting for alms and broken meats, were crowds of beggars, sitting and lying about in the sun, with their eyes ever on the latch to be first when it was lifted for the daily dole. And again, round the gate were many men of all sorts, suitors, as we deemed for some favour at the hands of bishop or abbot-- for the Abbot of Glastonbury was nigh as powerful as Ealhstan himself, in his own town at least.

When we came among these we were told that we must bide our time, for audience was not given but at stated hours. And one man, grumbling, said that that was not Ealhstan's way in his own place at Sherborne, for there the doors were open ever.

But I knew that my business might not wait, and so, after a little of this talk, went up to the gate and thundered thereon in such sort that the wicket opened, and the porter's face looked through it angrily enough, and he would have bidden us begone, for war and travel had stained us both, so that doubtless we were in no better case, as to looks, than the crowd that pressed after us--very quietly, indeed-- to hear the parley.

One difference in our looks there was, however, which made the porter silent--we wore mail and swords, and at that he seemed to stare in wonder.

Then I held up the ring and said, "Messages from Osric the Sheriff."

Whereupon the wicket closed suddenly, and there was a sound of unbarring, and the door opened and we were let in, the rest, who must wait, grumbling loudly at the preference shown to us, while the beggars, who had roused at the sound of the hinges creaking, went back whining in their disappointment.

Then one came and bade us follow him, and we were led into the abbey hall and there waited for a little. There were a few monks about, passing and repassing, but they paid no attention to us, and we, too, were silent in that quiet place. Only a great fire crackled at one end of the hall, else there would have been no noise at all. It was, I thought, a strangely peaceful place into which to bring news of war and tumult.

Then I thought of Ealhstan the Bishop, as he had seemed to me when he judged me, and that seemed years ago, nor could I think of myself as the same who had stood a prisoner before him. So I wondered if I should seem the same to him.

Now it is strange that of Eanulf, the mighty ealdorman who had pronounced my doom, I thought little at all, but as of one who was by the bishop. All that day's doings seemed to have been as a dream, wherein I and Wulfhere had living part with this bishop, while the rest, Eanulf and Matelgar and the others, were but phantoms standing by.

Maybe this is not so wonderful, for the doom was the doom of the Moot, and spoken by Eanulf as its mouthpiece, and that passed on my body only. And Matelgar had found a new place in my thoughts, but Wulfhere was my friend, and the bishop had spoken to my heart, so that his words and looks abode there.

Then the servant cut short my thoughts, and led us to the bishop, bidding me unhelm first.

He sat in a wide chamber, with another most venerable-looking man at the same table. And all the walls were covered with books, and on the table, too, lay one or two great ones, open, and bright with gold and crimson borderings, and great litters on the pages. But those things I saw presently, only the bishop first of all, sitting quietly and very upright in his great chair, dressed in a long purple robe, and with a golden cross hanging on his breast.

And for a moment as I looked at him, I remembered the day of the Moot, and my heart rose up, and I was ready to hide my face for minding the shame thereof.

But he looked at me curiously, and then all of a sudden smiled very kindly and said:

"Heregar, my son, are you the messenger?"

And I knelt before him on one knee, and held out the ring for him to take, and he did so, laying it on the table before him--for my errand was in hand yet.

"Then," he said, "things are none so ill with you, my son," and he smiled gravely; "but do your errand first, and afterwards we will speak of that."

So I rose up, and standing before him, told him plainly all that had befallen, though there was no need for me to say aught of myself in the matter, except that, flying with the lady, Osric had chosen me to bear the message of defeat and danger.

And the while I spoke the bishop's face grew very grave, but he said nothing till I ended by saying that Wulfhere could tell him of the fight.

Then he bade Wulfhere speak, being anxious to know the worst, as it seemed to me. But the old man with him was weeping, and his hands shook sorely.

Now into what Wulfhere told, my name seemed to come often, for he began with the first landing at Watchet, and my bearing the war arrow, and so forward to the firing of the huts at Stert, to the rallying on Cannington Hill, and our flight, and how Osric sent for me.

Then said the bishop, "Is that the worst?"

And Wulfhere was fain to answer that he feared not, telling of the smoke clouds we had seen, and what he judged therefrom.

"Aye," said the bishop, as it were to himself and looking before him as one who sees that which he is told of, "we saw the like after Charnmouth, and let them have their way. Now must we wait, trembling, for Osric's next messenger."

But as for me, though the old man was sorely terrified, as one might see, I thought there was little trembling on the bishop's part, though he spoke of it. Rather did he seem to speak in scorn of such as would so wait.

"Tell me now," he went on presently, "how the men rallied, and with what spirit, on the hill where Heregar stayed them?"

"Well and bravely," answered Wulfhere, "so that the Danes drew back, forming up hastily lest there should be an attack on them; but none was made."

Then the bishop's eyes flashed, and I thought to myself that I would he had been there. Surely he would have swept the Danes back to their ships, and I think that was in Wulfhere's mind also, for he said:

"We want a leader who can see these things. No blame to Osric therein, for it was his first fight."

Then the bishop laughed softly in a strange way, though his eyes still flashed, and he seemed to put the matter by.

"Truly," said he, "with you, Wulfhere, to advise, and myself to ask questions, and Heregar to prevent our running away, I think we might do great things. Well, there is Eanulf, who fought at Charnmouth."

So saying he rose up, and clapped his hands loudly. The old man had fallen to telling his beads, and paid no attention to him or us any longer, doubtless dreaming of the burning of his abbey over his head, unless some stronger help was at hand than that of the three men before him.

A lay brother came in to answer the bishop's summons.

"Take these thanes to the refectory," he said, "and care for them with all honour. In two hours I will speak with them again, or sooner, if Osric's messenger comes."

"I am no thane," said Wulfhere, not willing to be mistaken.

"I am Bishop of Sherborne," said he, smiling in an absent way, and waving his hand for us to go.

So we went, and thereafter were splendidly treated as most honoured guests, even to the replacing of the broad hat which Wulfhere had gotten from the franklin by a plain steel helm, with other changes of garment, for which we were most glad.

Now as we bathed and changed, I found that letter which Leofwine the hermit priest had given me, and I prayed the brother to give it to the bishop at some proper moment, and he took it away with him. I had forgotten it in the greater business.

While we ate and drank, and talked of how to reach Eanulf the Ealdorman, the brother came back and brought us a message, saying:

"The bishop bids you rest here in peace. He has sent messengers to Eanulf, bidding him come here in all haste to speak with him and you."

So I asked where he was, and the brother said that he lay at Wells, which pleased Wulfhere, who said that he would be here shortly, and that we were in luck, seeing that he wanted another good night's rest; and indeed so did I, sorely, though that I might yet stay near Alswythe was better still.

Before the two hours the bishop had set, there was a clamour in the great yard, and we thought the messenger from Osric had surely come. And so it was, for almost directly the bishop sent for us, and we were taken back to the same chamber. But he was alone now, and motioned us to seats beside him to one side.

Then they brought in a thane whom I did not know, and he said he was a messenger from Osric, laying a letter on the table at the same time. I saw that his armour was battle stained, and that he looked sorely downcast.

Not so the bishop as he read, for that which was written he had already expected, and he never changed his set look. Once he read the letter through, and then again aloud for us to hear. Thus it ran after fit greeting:

"Now what befell in the first fight you know or shall know shortly from our trusty messenger Heregar, by whom the flight was stayed from that field, on the Hill of Cannington. And this was well done. So, seeing that the Danes had drawn off, I myself, foolishly deeming the matter at an end, left three hundred men on that hill to watch the Danes back to their ships, and returned to the town, there to muster again the men who were sound, and, if it were possible, to lead them on the Danes as they went on board again to depart. For the men, save those of Bridgwater, would not bide on the hill, but came back, saving the Danes would surely depart. And, indeed, I also thought so; but wrongly. For even as I talked with Heregar of his own affairs, news came of a fresh attack, whereon I sent him to you, fearing the worst, for the men on the hill were few, and those in the town seeming of little spirit.

"Now when I came three parts of the way to Cannington, our men there were sped and driven back on us. Whereupon I could no longer hold together any force, and whither the men are scattered I know not. Scarcely could I save the holy women and the monks, for even as they fled under guard into the Quantock woods, and so to go beyond the hills, the houses of Bridgwater next the Danes were burning.

"Now am I with two hundred men on Brent, and wait either for the Danes to depart, or for orders from yourself or the Ealdorman Eanulf, to whom I pray you let this letter be sent in haste after that you have read it."

So it ended with salutations, and when he had read it, the bishop folded it slowly and looked at the thane, who shrugged his broad shoulders and said:

"True words, Lord Bishop, and all told."

"It is what I expected," said Ealhstan, "these two thanes told me it was like to be thus."

"Surely," answered the thane. "What else?"

The bishop looked at him and asked him his name.

"Wislac, the Thane of Gatehampton by the Thames, am I," he said. "A stranger here, having come on my own affairs to Bridgwater, and so joining in the fight. Also, Osric's thanes having trouble enough on hand, I rode with this letter."

"Thanks therefor," said the bishop. "I see that you fought also in a place where blows were thick."

"Aye, in the first fight," said Wislac. "As for the second, being with Osric, I never saw that."

"Did you stay on the hill where men rallied?"

"That did I, as any man would when the saints came to stay us. Otherwise I had surely halted at Bridgwater, or this side thereof," answered the strange thane, with a smile that was bitter enough.

Now the bishop had not heard that tale of the saint on a white horse; but he was quick enough, and glanced aside at me. Whereupon Wislac the Thane looked also, and straightway his mouth opened, and he stared at me. Then, being nowise afraid of the bishop, or, as it seemed, of saints, he said aloud, seemingly to himself:

"Never saw I bishop before. Still, I knew that they were blessed with visions; but that live saints should sit below their seat, I dreamt not!" and so he went on staring at me.

So the bishop, for all his trouble, could but smile, and asked him if he saw a vision.

"Surely," he said, "this is the saint who stayed us on yonder hill."

"Nay, that is Heregar the Thane, messenger of Osric."

"Then," said Wislac, "let me tell you, Heregar the Thane, that one of the saints, and I think a valiant one, is mightily like you. Whereby you are the more fortunate."

Now for all the mistake I could not find a word to say, and was fain to thank him for the good word on my looks. Yet he went on looking at me now and then in a puzzled sort of way. And the bishop seemed to enjoy his wonderment, but was in no mind to enlighten him.

Presently the bishop bade Wislac sit down, and then he took up Osric's ring that I had given him, and also another which lay beside it on the table--silver also, with some device on it, like that I had worn.

"See, thanes," he said, "have you three a mind to stay with me for a while and be my council in this matter? For I am here without a fighting man of my own to speak with."

Now this was what I would most wish, and I said so, eagerly and with thanks.

And Wislac said that he was surely in good company, and having nought to call him home would gladly stay also.

Then said the bishop, "Stranger you are, friend Wislac, and therefore wear this ring of Osric's, that men may pay heed to you as his friend and mine; and do you, Heregar, wear this of mine that men may know you for bishop's man, and so respect your word."

So was I put under the bishop's protection, and he would answer for my presence in Wessex to all and any. That was good, and I felt a free man again in truth, for here was no errand that would end, as Osric's was ended, when I had seen Ean-ulf.

Now Wulfhere had not spoken, and the bishop asked him if he too would not stay.

"Ay, lord," answered Wulfhere, "gladly; but you spoke of thanes only."

"When the Bishop of Sherborne names one as a thane," said Ealhstan, smiling, "men are apt to hold him as such. But only to the worthy are such words spoken. Now, friend Wulfhere, I have heard of you at Charnmouth fight, and also there is more in Osric's letter than I have read to you. So if you will be but a bishop's land-less thane, surely you shall be one"

Then Wulfhere grew red with pleasure, and rising up, did obeisance to the bishop for the honour, and the bishop called us two others to witness that the same was given.

"Now is my council set," he said, "I to ask questions, and you to advise."

So for a long two hours we sat and told him all we knew of those Danes, I of the ships, and Wulfhere and Wislac of numbers, and Wulfhere of their ways in raiding a country, for this he had seen before, in Dorset, and also in Ireland, as he told us, in years gone by.

That night we were treated as most honoured guests of the bishop's own fol-lowing, and early in the morning the bishop sent for me, before mass. Once again I found him alone in that room of his, and all he said to me I cannot write down. But I found that Leofwine the hermit had told him of how I had taken counsel of him and abided by it, even as Ealhstan himself had bidden me; and, moreover, that Osric had written in his letter of what I had been able to do against the Danes, and of Matelgar's last words concerning me. And for that remembrance of me, accord-ing to his promise, even when writing of far greater matters, I am ever grateful to the good sheriff.

So, because of these things known, Ealhstan spoke to me as a most loving fa-ther, praising me where it seemed that praise was due, and reproving me for the many things of deed and thought that were evil. And I told him freely and fully all that had passed from the time I left the hill of Brent till when I had seen the signals of the vikings from above Watchet, and bore the war arrow to Matelgar. The rest he knew in a way; but I opened all my heart to him, he drawing all from me most gently, till at last I came to my dream of Matelgar, and my wish that for me he might rest in peace.

"It is not all forgiveness, Heregar, my son," he said presently. "There is love for Alsywthe, and pride in yourself, and thought of Matelgar's failure, which have at least brought you to a beginning of it. But true forgiveness comes slowly, and many a long day shall it be before that has truly come."

And I knew that maybe he was right, and asked his help; whereupon that was freely given, and in such sort that all my life long I must mind the words he said, and love him in the memory.

When all that was said he would have me hear mass with him, as though I needed urging. And there, too, were Wulfhere and Wislac; and that mass in the great abbey was the most wonderful I ever heard.

After that we three went out into the town, and Wislac and I marvelled at everything. Then we went to the nunnery gates and asked how our charges fared, and then saw to our steeds. There was the collier, working as a groom with the other men, and he told me that he was learning his new trade fast, but would fain walk ever, rather than ride, having fallen many times from the abbess' mule, which he had bestridden in anxiety to learn. Whether the mule was the better for this lesson I doubt.

When we went back to the abbey Eanulf had come, and with him many thanes. And I feared to meet these somewhat, for they might have been among the Moot, and would know me. Yet Ealhstan had foreseen this, and one was posted at the door to meet me, bidding me aside privately, since the bishop needed me.

Wulfhere and Wislac went into the hall and left me, therefore, and I was taken to a chamber where were six or seven lay brethren, who asked me many things about the fight, and specially at last about the saint who had appeared. And that was likely to be a troublesome question for me, as I could not claim to have been the one so mistaken; but another struck in, saying that there were many strange portents about, for that a fiend had appeared bodily from the marsh and had devoured a child, in Sedgemoor. Now it seems that fiends are rarer than saints among these holy men, and they forgot the first wonder and ran on about the second, not thinking that I could have told them of that also. And at last one fetched a great book, as I thought in some secrecy, and made thereout nothing more nor less than parts of the song of Beowulf itself, and all about Grendel, which pleased us all well, and so we were quiet enough, listening.

And it happened that while we were all intent on this reading (and I never heard one read as brother Guthlac read to us) the sub-prior came in to call me, and pulling back the hangings of the doorway, stood listening, where I could see him.

First of all he looked pleased to find his people so employed. Then when the crash of the fighting verses came to his ears he started a little, and looked round. The good brothers were like to forget their frocks, for their fists were clenched and their eyes sparkled, and their teeth were set, and verily I believe each man of them thought himself one of Beowulf's comrades, if not the hero himself.

Whereupon the sub-prior and I were presently grinning at one another.

"Ho!" said he, all of a sudden. "Now were I Swithun, where would you heathens spend tonight? Surely in the cells!"

Then for a moment they thought Grendel had indeed come, such power has verse like this in the mouth of a good reader, and they started up, one and all.

And the reader saw who it was, and that there was no hiding the book from him, so they stood agape and terrified, for by this time the good man had managed to look mighty stern.

"Good Father," said I, seeing that someone must needs speak, "I am but a fighting man, and the brothers were considering my weakness."

"H'm," said the sub-prior, seeming in great wrath. "Is there no fighting to be read from Holy Writ that you must take these pagan vanities from where you ought not? Go to! Yet, by reason of your care for the bishop's thane, your penance shall be light now and not heavy hereafter. Brother Guthlac shall read aloud in refectory today the story of David and Goliath, and you brother," pointing to one, "that of Ahab at Ramoth, and you, of Joshua at Jericho," and so he went on till each had a chapter of war assigned him, and I thought it an easy penance.

"But," he added, "and until all these are read, your meals shall be untasted before you."

Then the brothers looked at one another, for it was certain that all this reading would last till the meal must be left for vespers.

Then the sub-prior bade the reader take back the book and go to his own cell, and beckoning me, we passed out and left the brothers in much dismay, not knowing what should befall them from the abbot when he heard.

So I ventured to tell the sub-prior how this came about, and he smiled, saying that he should not tell Tatwine the Abbot, for the brothers were seldom in much fault, and that maybe it was laudable to search even pagan books for the manners of fiends, seeing that forewarned was forearmed.

Then he said that surely he wished (but this I need tell none else) that he had been there in my place to hear Guthlac read it. Also that he was minded to make the old rhyme more Christian-like, if he could, writing parts of it afresh. And this he has done since, so that any man may read it; but it is not so good as the old one [ix].

Now we came to the bishop's chamber, and he went in, calling me after him in a minute or so. I could hear Ealhstan's voice and that of another as I waited outside.

The other was Eanulf the Ealdorman, and as I entered he rose up and faced me.

"So, Heregar," he said, "you are bishop's man now, and out of my power. I am glad of it," and so saying he reached me out his hand and wrung mine, and looked very friendly as he did so.

"I have heard of your doings," he said, "and thank you for them. And I will see this matter of yours looked into, for I think, as the bishop believes, that there has been a plot against you for plain reasons enough. However, that must stand over as yet. But come with me to the hall and I will right you with the thanes there."

At that I thanked him, knowing that things were going right with me, and the bishop smiled, as well pleased, but said nothing, as Eanulf took me by the arm, and we went together to the great hall, where the thanes, some twenty of them, were talking together. At once I saw several whose faces had burnt themselves, as it were, into my mind at the Moot; but none of Matelgar's friends among them.

They were quiet when their leader went in, and he wasted no time, but spoke in his own direct way.

"See here, thanes; here is Heregar, whom we outlawed but the other day. Take my word and Ealhstan's and Osric's for it that there was a mistake. We know now that there is no truer man, for he has proved it, as some of you know-he being the man who lit the huts at Stert in face of the Danes, and being likewise the Saint of

Cannington--"

"Aye, it is so," said several voices, and others laughed. Then, like honest Saxons as they were, they came crowding and laughing to shake hands with an outlawed saint, as one said; so that I was overdone almost with their kindness, and knew not what to say or do.

But Eanulf pushed me forward among them, saying that I, being bishop's man, was no more concern of his, outlaw or no outlaw, and that saints were beyond him. So he too laughed, and went back to the bishop; and I found Wulfhere and Wislac, and soon I was one of my own sort again, and the bad past seemed very far away.

But Wislac looked at me and said: "You have spoilt a fine tale I had to take home with me; but maybe I need not tell the ending. Howbeit, I always did hold that there was none so much difference between a fighting saint and one of ourselves."

And that seemed to satisfy him.

CHAPTER XII. THE GREAT LEVY.

It was not long before Eanulf made up his mind to action, and he was closeted with the bishop all that morning. Then, after the midday meal, he called a council of all who were there, and we sat in the great hall to hear his plans.

Ealhstan came with him, and these two sat at the upper end of the hall, and we on the benches round the walls, for the long tables had been cleared.

When all was ready, Eanulf stood up and told the thanes, for some were men who had had no part in Osric's levy, all about the fighting, and how it had ended. And having done that, he asked for the advice of such as would have aught to say.

Very soon an old thane rose up and said that he thought all would be well if forces were so posted as to prevent the Danes coming beyond the land they then held.

And several growled assent to that; and one said that Danes bided in one place no long time, but would take ship again and go elsewhere.

That, too, seemed to please most, and I saw Eanulf bite his lip, for he was a man who loved action. And Wulfhere, too, shifted in his seat, as if impatient.

Then they went back to the first proposal, and began to name places where men might be posted to keep the Danes in Parret valley at least, till they went away.

Then at last Wulfhere grew angry, and rose up, looking very red.

"And what think you will Parret valley be like when they have done their will therein? Does no man remember the going back to his place when these strangers had bided in it for a while, after they beat us in Dorset?"

There were two thanes who had lands in that part, and they flushed, so that one might easily know they remembered; but they said naught.

Then Eanulf spake, very plainly:

"I am for raising the levy of Somerset again, and stronger, and driving them out; but I cannot do it without your help."

Then there was silence, and the thanes looked at one another for so long that I waxed impatient, and being headstrong, maybe, got up and spoke:

"Landless I am, and maybe not to be hearkened to, but nevertheless I will say what it seems to me that a man should say. Into this land of peace these men from over seas have come wantonly, slaying our friends, burning our houses, driving our cattle, making such as escape them take to the woods like hunted wild beasts. Where is Edred the Thane? Where is Matelgar? Where twenty others you called friends? Dead by Combwich, and none to bury them. The Danes have their arms, the wolves their bodies. Is no vengeance to be taken for this? Or shall the Danes sail away laughing, saying that the hearts of the Saxons are as water?"

Then there rose an angry growl at that, and I was glad to hear it. So was Eanulf, as it seemed. And Wulfhere got up and stood beside me and spoke.

"This is good talk, and now I will add a word. Why came back the Danes here? Because after we were beaten before, we let them do their worst, and hindered them not; therefore come they back even now--aye, and if we drive them not from us, hither will they come yet again, till we may not call the land our own from year to year. I say with the ealdorman, let us up and drive them out, showing them what Saxons are made of. What? Are we done fighting after they have scattered one hastily gathered levy? Shame there is none to us in being so beaten once, but I hold it shame to let them so easily have the mastery."

Then there was a murmur, but not all of assent; though I could see that many would side with us. Whereon Wislac rose up slowly, and looking round, said:

"I am a stranger, but having been present at the beating the other day, yonder, am minded to see if I may yet go home on the winning side. And it would be shame, even as these two thanes have said, not to give a guest a chance to have his pleasure. I pray you, thanes, pluck up spirit, and follow the ealdorman."

Now, though Wislac's words seemed idle at the beginning, there was that in his last words which brought several of the younger thanes to their feet, looking angrily at him, and one asked if he meant to call that assembly "nidring".

"Not I," said Wislac, smiling peacefully, "seeing that you have done naught to deserve that foul name; but being a beaten man, as I said, I need a chance to prove that I am not 'nidring' myself, so please you."

And they could not take offence at his tone, yet they saw well what he meant; and this in the end touched them very closely, for they were in the same case as he, but with more right, being of Somerset, to wipe out their defeat. But maybe there would have been a quarrel if Eanulf had not spoken.

"Peace, thanes," he said. "Heregar is right, and we must avenge our dead. Wulfhere is right, and for the land's sake we must give these Danes a lesson to bide at home. Wislac is right, and this defeat must be wiped out. Now say if you will help me to raise the levy afresh?"

"Aye, we will," said the thanes, but there was not that heartiness in their tones that one might have looked for.

In truth, though, it was no want of courage, but the thought of the easier plan of waiting, that held them back.

Then Ealhstan the Bishop rose up and faced us all, with his eyes shining, and his right hand gripping his crosier so tightly that his knuckles shone white.

"What, my sons, shall it be said of you, as it is said of us Dorset folk, that you let the Danes bide in your land and work their worst on you and yours? I tell you that since we went back and saw, as we still see, their track over our homes, our folk burn to take revenge on them; and I, being what I am, think no wrong of counselling revenge on heathen folk. Listen, for ye are men."

And then he told us in burning words such a tale of what must be were these heathen to have their way, such things that he himself had seen and known after Charnmouth fight, that we would fain at last be up and drive them away without waiting for the levy.

And at last he said:

"Eanulf, this will I do. I will gather the Dorset levy and lead them to your help, and so will we make short work of these heathen."

Then all the thanes shouted that they would not be behind in the matter; and so their cool Saxon blood was fired to that white rage which is quenched but in victory or death.

Now after that there was talk of nothing but of making the levy as soon as might be, and Eanulf, thanking everyone, and most of all the bishop, straightway gave his orders; and before that night the war arrow was speeding through all Somerset and Dorset likewise, and word was sent to Osric and the other sheriffs that the gathering place named was at the hill of Brent.

Now of those days that followed there is little to say. The other thanes left, each to gather his own men, vowing vengeance on the Danes; but before they went there was hardly one who did not seek out Wulfhere, Wislac, and myself, and in some way or another tell us that we had spoken right. One fiery young thane, indeed, was minded to fight Wislac, but the Mercian turned the quarrel very skilfully, and in the end agreed with the thane that the matter should be settled by the number of Danes each should slay, "which," said Wislac, "will be as good sport and more profitable than pounding one another, and quite as good proof that neither of us may be held nidring."

So that ended very well.

But every day came in reports, brought by fugitives, of the Danes and their doings, which made our blood boil. At last came one who brought a message for myself, could I be found. It was from the aunt of Alswythe, the Prioress of Bridgwater, telling of her safety and that of her nuns, at Taunton. And I begged the bishop to let me tell this good news to Alswythe, and so gained speech with her once more. Yet would the abbess be present, reading the while; but I might tell my love all that had befallen me, and she rejoiced, bidding me go fight and win myself renown in the good cause of my own country.

And when I left her I felt that I must indeed be strong for the sake of her, and by reason of her words, which would be in my mind ever.

Now one day when I went to see the horses and ride out with Wulfhere and Wislac, the collier came and hung about, seeming to wish to ask somewhat. And when I noticed this and bade him speak, he prayed me that I would give him arms, and let him follow me to the coming fighting. Arms, save those I wore, I had none, but I promised him such as I could buy him with what remained of the money I had found, which might be enough, seeing that we lived at free quarters with the bishop, and had little expense. As for the other money, I left that with the abbess after I had seen Alswythe, for it was less mine than hers.

But I asked Dudda if he were able to use a sword. Whereupon he grinned, and said that Brother Guthlac tended the abbot's mule, and had taught him much when he came to the stables daily. He also showed me a bruised arm and broken head in token of hard play with the ash plant between them.

"Here is the said Guthlac," said Wulfhere; and there was the reader of Beowulf coming, with frock and sleeves tucked up, from out the stables. So I called him, and asked him to try a bout with the collier, telling him why.

At first he denied all knowledge of carnal warfare, but I reminded him of his reading of Beowulf, saying that, if he knew naught of fighting, the verses would have had none of that fire in them. So, in the end, they went to it, and I saw that Guthlac was well used to sword play, and was satisfied also with his pupil.

Then I asked Guthlac whence he got his skill in arms, and why he was shut up thus inside four walls.

"Laziness, Thane," he answered, telling me nothing of the first matter at all. Nor would he. But I found afterwards that he had been lamed once, and tended by the monks, and so had bided in the abbey, liking the life, though he had been a stout housecarle to some thane or other.

Then Wislac must ask him if there were any more of his sort in the abbey, and seeing that we meant no harm, and looking on me as an ally in that matter of the reading, he said there were five more, "whom Heregar the Thane knew, if he would remember, reading certain Scriptures at supper time."

And I found that these six kindred spirits had managed to get themselves told off to amuse me while I waited that day, so that they might hear of the fighting.

So we laughed and rode out, and I thought no more of Guthlac and his brethren till the time came when I remembered them gladly.

All day long during that week came pouring in the Dorset levies in answer to the bishop's summons. Hard and wiry men they were, and as I could well see, a very much harder set than Osric's first levy, for these were veterans. Ealhstan's word had gone out that all men who would wipe out the defeat of Charnmouth should gather to him, and these were the men who had fought there, and only longed to try their strength again against their conquerors of that disastrous day.

Day by day, also, would Ealhstan go out into the marketplace, and there speak burning words to them, bidding them remember the days gone by, and the valour of their fathers who won the land for them, and to have ever in mind that this war was not of Christian against Christian, but against heathen men who were profaning the houses of God wherever they came.

Many more things did he say, ever finding something fresh wherewith to stir their courage, but ever, also, did he bid them remember how the Danes had won by discipline more than courage, and to pay heed to that as their leaders bade them.

Also, day by day, he bade the thanes who had seen fighting, train their men as well as they might, and they worked well at that. Moreover, he could teach them much, reading to us at times from a great Latin book of the wars of Caesar such things as seemed like to be useful, putting it into good Saxon as he went on.

Then, as the week drew to an end, there began to be questions as to who should be leader of the Dorset men. And many said that Osric should be the man, for he was an Ealdorman of Dorset. But when the bishop sent to Brent for him, and asked him to lead his men, Osric doubted; and what he said to the other thanes, and to us three, made them send us to the bishop with somewhat to ask.

So we, finding him ever ready to hear what was wanted, put the question to him plainly as they had bidden us. And that was, that he himself should lead the levy of Dorset.

Now Tatwine, the old abbot, sat with him and heard this, and straightway he began to tremble, and cry out that such work was unfit for a bishop.

So the bishop said to me, very quietly, but with a look in his eyes which seemed to show that this was what he longed for:

"Heregar, my son, go and tell the thanes what the abbot says, and ask if they will go without me."

All the thanes were waiting to hear the bishop's answer to our request, and I told them this, and they knew at once what answer to give, for they said, or Osric said for them, while all applauded:

"We will not go against these heathens unless the bishop leads us. Else must Somerset fight her own battles."

So with that word I went back to the bishop, and told him.

"So, Tatwine, my brother, you see how it is. Needs must that I go, else were it shame to us that heathen men should have freedom in a Christian land."

But Tatwine groaned, and, maybe knowing the bishop well, said no more.

Then Ealhstan bade him remember all the saints who had warred against the heathen, and were held blameless--nay, rather, the holier.

"Therefore," said he, "I am in good company, and will surely go."

Whereupon Tatwine rose up and went out, saying that he should go to the abbey and seek protection for the bishop, and men say he bided there almost night and day, praying until all was past. Certainly I saw him no more in his accustomed places, save at mass.

When he had gone the bishop smiled a little, looking after him, and then spoke to us.

"I may tell my council that this is what I should love. Nevertheless, it will not be I who lead, but you three. For the counsel must be Wulfhere's, and the coolness Wislac's, and the rest Heregar's, who will by no means bide that we run away. Now, I think that you three will make a good leader of me."

On that we thanked him for his words, and we followed him out to the hall. And there the thanes shouted and cheered as he came, and still more when he prayed them to follow him to victory or a warrior's death. And that they swore to do, not loudly, but in such sort that none could mistake that they would surely do so.

Then he bade them muster their men by the first light in the morning, and so he would lead them first of all to Brent, to join the ealdorman. And Osric should be his second in command.

That pleased all, and soon we were left alone with him again, but we could hear outside the cheering of men now and then, as some thane gathered his following and told them the name of their leader.

So we three went out presently and saw to our horses, and then I was wondering about arms for Dudda, for I had left the matter too long, and it seemed there were few weapons remaining for sale in the town by reason of men of the levy buying or borrowing what they lacked in equipment. And the poor fellow hung about sadly, thinking he should find none in the end, and swearing he would follow me even had he naught but a quarterstaff in his hand.

But when we went back to the abbey, the bishop sent for us, and we were taken into a room we had not seen before, and there on the table were laid out three suits of mail, helmets, and arms.

"Now," said Ealhstan, as he saw our eyes go, as a man's eyes will, straight to these things, "if you thanes are not too proud to accept such as I can give, let me arm you, and tell you where you shall bear these arms."

And that was what we longed for, for as yet we had no post in the levy, and we told him as much.

"That is well," he answered. "See, Wislac, here is bright steel armour and helm and shield for you. Sword also, if you need it, for maybe you will scarce part from your own tried weapon?"

But Wislac smiled at that, and took hold of his sword hilt, loosening the strings which bound it to the sheath. There were but eight inches of blade left, and these were sorely notched.

"Aha!" quoth the bishop, "now know I why Wislac thought well to stop fighting the other day," which pleased the Mercian well enough.

"Then, Wulfhere," went on Ealhstan, "here is this black armour and helm and shield for you, and sword or axe as you will."

And Wulfhere thanked him, taking the axe, as his own sword was good.

"Now, Heregar, my son, this is yours," said the bishop, looking kindly at me.

And as I looked I thought I had never seen more beautiful arms. No better were they than the other two suits, for all three were of good Sussex ring mail as to the byrnies, [x] while the boar-crested helms were of hammered steel.

But mine was silver white, with gold collar and gold circles round the arms. Gold, too, was the boar-crest of the helm, and gold the circle round the head, and to me it seemed as I looked that this was too good. And Ealhstan knew my thoughts and answered them.

"Black for the man of dark counsel, bright steel for the warrior, and silver-bright armour for the man who brings back hope when all seems lost."

"That is good," said Wislac. "Now read us the meaning of the gold thereon also," for he seemed to see that the bishop had some meaning in that, whereat the bishop smiled.

"Gold for trust," he said, "and for the man who shall be honoured."

"That is well also," said Wulfhere, and Wislac nodded gravely.

"Now," said the bishop, "I will put Heregar out of my council for a minute, so that he may not speak nor hear. Tell me, Thanes both, if it will be well to give Heregar the place whereto men shall rally in need?"

"Aye, surely," they said. "We know he can fill that place."

"Then shall he bear my standard," said the bishop, "and none will gainsay it," and so he turned to me.

"Now, Heregar, may you hear this decision. Standard bearer to me shall you be, and I know you will bear it well and bravely. And these two, your friends and mine, shall stand to right and left of you, and six stout carles may you choose from the levy to stand before and behind you. And whom you choose I will arm alike, that all may know them."

Now knew I not what to say or do, but I knelt before the bishop and kissed his hand, and so he laid it on my head and blessed me, bidding me speak no words of thanks, but only deserve them from him.

Now there was a little silence after this, and Wislac, being ever ready, broke it for us,

"Much do I marvel," he said, "that these suits of armour should be so exactly fitting to each of us. Surely there is some magic in it."

"Only the magic of a wearied man's sleep, and of a good weapon smith," said the bishop, laughing. "One measured your mail, byrnie and helm both, as you slept. We have lay brethren apt for every craft."

And that reminded me of Brother Guthlac, and a thought came to me.

"Father," I said, "six men have you bidden me choose, and I know none of the Dorset men. Yet there are six lay brethren here who have been warriors, of whom brother Guthlac is one, and if they may march against heathen men, I pray you let me have them."

Now that the Bishop seemed to find pleasant, as though he knew something of those lovers of war songs, and answered that he wot not if Tatwine would let them go. But, in any case, he would choose men for me of the best, and that we all thought well, knowing in what spirit he would put those men whom he should choose.

So he bade us go, taking our arms with us, and we, thanking him, went out. But I found my collier, and showed him the arms I had been wearing, saying they should be his, and then took him, rejoicing, into the town. There I bought him, after some search, a plain, good sword and target, which he bore to his lodgings to scour and gaze at for the rest of the day.

CHAPTER XIII. A MESSAGE FROM THE DEAD.

How shall I tell what it was like when the bishop, standing aloft at the head of the abbey steps with all the monks round him, gave into my hands, as I knelt, his standard to bear at the head of his men?

Very early in the morning it was, and all the roofs were golden in bright sunlight, and the men, drawn up in a hollow square fronting the abbey, were silent and attentive as mass was sung in the great church, so that the sound of the chanting came out to them through the open doors. And when the sacring [xi] bell rang, as though a wave went along the ranks, all knelt, and there was a clash and ring of steel, and then silence for a space, very wonderful.

Then came out, when mass was said, bishop, and thanes, and monks, and there gave me the banner, Wulfhere and Wislac kneeling on either side of me, and behind us those six stout housecarles whom the bishop had chosen and armed for me. So the banner was given and blessed, and I rose up, grasping the golden-hafted cross from which it hung, and lifted it that all might see.

Then was a great shout from all the men, and swords were drawn and brandished on every side, and, without need of command, all the Dorset host swore to follow it even to the death. And that was good to hear.

But as for me, my thoughts were more than I may write, but it seems to me that they were as those of Saint George when he rode out to slay the dragon in the old days, so great were they.

After that a little wait, and then the horses; and the bishop mounted a great bay charger, managing him as a master. And to me was brought my white horse by the collier, looking a grim fighting man enough in his arms, and to Wulfhere and Wislac black and gray steeds given by Ealhstan himself.

Now the bishop rode, followed by us, to the centre of the levy, and again a great shout rose up even mightier than that first, and when it ended he spoke to the men as he was wont to speak but even yet more freely, and then put himself at their head, and so began the march to Brent. And all the town was out to see us go, never doubting of our victory, nor thinking of how few might return of all that long line of sturdy and valiant fighting men.

When we were clear of the town at last, and went, the men singing as they marched, down the ancient green lanes that had seen our forefathers' levies and the Roman legions alike, I had time to look around me at my own following, being conscious in some way that, mixed up as it were with the war song, there had been the sound of the droning of a chant as by monks close by me. And I could see no monks near. The thanes were riding round and after the bishop, who came next me as I led the way with the standard, and Ealhstan indeed had on his robes; but there was a stiffness about him, and a glint of steel also, when a breeze shifted the loose fold of his garments, that seemed to say that his was not all peaceful gear.

Just behind me, as I rode with Wulfhere and Wislac to right and left, came my six men, big powerful housecarles, all in black armour and carrying red and black shields, and with a red cross on their helms' fronts. And the squarest of these six, he who seemed to be their leader, looked up at me, when I turned again, with a grin that I seemed to know. So I took closer notice of him, and lo! it was Guthlac, the reader of Beowulf, and the other five were his brethren. Small wonder that I had not recognized the holy men in their war gear, so little looked they like the peaceful brethren who had walked in the abbey cloisters.

With them was my collier, keeping step and holding himself with the best of them, and I thought that they would be seven hardy Danes who should overmatch my standard guard. So I was well content with the bishop's choice for me.

Now of that march to Brent, and the meeting there with the Somerset levy, there is no need to tell. But by the time we marched from thence against the Danes, there were five hundred men of Dorset, and near nine hundred of Somerset. Of the Danes some judged that there would be eight hundred or more, but if that was so, they were tried men, and our numbers were none too great. Moreover, we must separate, so as to drive them down to their ships, for they were spread over the country, burning and destroying on every side.

We lay but one night on Brent, while the leaders held counsel, and even as we sat gathered, we could see plainly the fires the Danes had lit, of burning hamlet and homestead, far and wide across the marshes of Parret. And the end of that council was that Eanulf should take his Somerset men up Parret valley, and so drive down the Danes, while Ealhstan should fall on them by Bridgwater as they came down, and so scatter them.

Therefore would the Somerset levy march very early, before light; while we should wait till the next night, unless word should come beforehand.

So we went to sleep. And as I slept in my place, with the standard flapping above me, and my comrades on either side and behind, it seemed to me that one came and waked me. And when I sat up and looked, thinking it was a messenger from the bishop, I saw that it was Matelgar.

Now this time I had no fear of him, and I waited for him to speak, just as though he had been before me in the flesh, for there seemed naught uncanny about the matter to me. And yet even at the moment that seemed strange, though it was so.

But for a while he looked not at me, but out over the low lands towards Parret mouth and Stert, shading his eyes with his hand as though it were broad noonday. And then he turned back to me and spoke.

"Heregar; I promised to stand by you again when the time came. Now I bid you go to Combwich hill, there to wait what betides. So, if you will do the bidding of the dead who has wronged you, but would now make amends, shall you thank me for this hereafter--aye, and not you only."

Then out over Parret he gazed again and faded from beside me, so that I could ask him nothing. Then knew I that I was awake, and that this had been no dream; for a great fear came on me for a little, knowing what I had seen to be not of this world. Yet all around me my comrades slept, and only round the rim of the trenched hill went the wakeful sentries, too far for speech--for we leaders were in the centre of the camp.

But presently I began to think less of the vision, and more of the words. And at first they seemed vain, for Combwich hill was over near to Stert; nor did I see how

I could reach the place without cutting through the Danes (who would doubtless leave a strong guard with the ships, and were also in and about Bridgwater), seeing that the river must be crossed.

Then as I turned over the matter, not doubting but that a message so given was sooth, and by no means lightly to be disregarded, I seemed to wake to a resolve concerning the meaning of the whole thing. What if I could win there under cover of darkness, and so fall on the Danish host as Eanulf drove them back and the bishop and Osric chased them to the ships?

That seemed possible, if only I could cross Parret with men enough, and unseen. I would ask Wulfhere and Wislac, when morning came, and so, if they could help, lay the matter before the bishop himself. So thinking I fell asleep again, peacefully enough, nor dreamt I aught.

With morning light that vision and the bidding to Combwich, and what I had thought thereon, seemed yet stronger. Very early the Somerset men went with Eanulf, and we of the bishop's levy only remained on Brent after the morning meal.

Then as we three stood on the edge of the hill, and looked out where Matelgar had looked, I told my two friends of his coming and of his words.

"Three things there are," said Wislac, "that hinder this ghost's business; namely, want of wings, uncertainty of darkness, and ignorance of the time when the Danes shall come."

"There are also three things that make for it, brother," said Wulfhere. "Namely: that men can swim, that there is no moon, and that the Danes are careless in their watch of the waste they leave behind them."

"Think you that the hill will be unguarded?" asked I, glad that Wulfhere did not put away the plan at once.

"Why should they guard it? There are Danes at the ships--though few, I expect, for we have been well beaten. And more in plenty from Parret to Quantocks, and no Saxon left between the two forces."

"Why not burn the ships then?" asked Wislac.

"Doubtless that could we, once over Parret," answered Wulfhere, "but what then? Away go the Danes through Somerset, burning and plundering even to Cornwall, and there bide till ships come, and then can be gone in safety. That is not what we need. We have to trap them and beat them here."

"So then, Wulfhere," I said, "think you that the plan is good?"

"Aye," he answered, "good enough; but not easy. Moreover, I doubt if the bishop would let his standard bearer part from him."

That was likely enough to stop all the plan; but yet I would lay it before Ealhstan, for it seemed to us that such a message might by no means go untold at least.

So we sought him, and asked for speech with him; and at that he laughed, saying that surely his council had the best right to that. Osric was with him, and the bishop told him how that we three had been his first advisers in this matter.

Then we sat down and I told Ealhstan all, asking nothing.

When I had ended, Osric looked at me, and said that the plan was venturesome; but no doubt possible to be carried out, and if so, by none better than myself, who knew every inch of that country. Then, thinking over it, as it were, he added that the woods beyond Matelgar's hall would shelter any force that must needs seek cover, so that, even were Combwich hill unsafe, there was yet a refuge whence attack could again be made.

Then Ealhstan, who had listened quietly, said that such messages were rare, but all the less to be despised. Therefore would he think thereof more fully.

"What," he asked, "is the main difficulty?"

I said that the crossing of Parret was like to be hard in any case; but at night and unobserved yet more so. But that, could we reach the farther bank, I could find places where we might lie in wait for a day, if need were, with many men.

Thereupon the bishop took that great book of Caesar's wars, and looked into it. But he seemed long in finding aught to meet that case, while we talked of one thing or another concerning it among ourselves.

At last he shut the book and said, very gravely: "I would that I could swim."

"I also, Father," said Wislac, "and why I cannot, save for sheer cowardice, I know not, having been brought up on Thames side, and never daring to go out of depth."

At that we were fain to laugh, so dismally did the broad-shouldered Mercian blame himself. But the bishop said that if I went, needs must that he came also. But he did not dissuade me in any way.

"Wulfhere the Counsellor," he said then, "have you no plan?"

"To cross the river?" answered the veteran. "Aye, many, if they may be managed. Rafts for those who cannot swim, surely."

Now I bethought me of the many boats that ever lay in the creek under Comb-wich, and wondered if any were yet whole. For if they were, surely one might swim over and bring one back. And that I said.

Then of a sudden, the bishop rose up, and seemed to have come to a decision, saying:

"See here, thanes; ever as we march to Bridgwater, we draw nearer Parret. Now by this evening, we shall be close over against this place Combwich, so that one may go thither and spy what there is to be done, and come back in good time and tell us if crossing may be made by raft or boat. Let this rest till then. But if it may be so, then I, and Heregar and his following, and two hundred men will surely cross, and wait for what may betide. For I think this plan is good."

So he would say no more of it then. And presently all his men were mustered, and we marched from Brent slowly along the way to Bridgwater.

CHAPTER XIV. ELGAH THE FISHER.

Now men have said that this plan of mine needed no ghost to set it forth, but is such that would enter the mind of any good leader. That might be so had there been one there who knew the country as I knew it, but there was not. And I was no general as was Eanulf. However that might be, I tell what happened to me in the matter, and sure am I that but for Matelgar's bidding I had never thought of this place or plan.

But once Ealhstan had heard thereof, the thought of it seemed ever better to him. And when we were fairly marching along the level towards Bridgwater he called me, and began to talk of that business of spying out the crossing place.

Now I too had been thinking of that same, and asked him to let me go at once, taking one man with me. Then would I rejoin him as best I might, and close to the place where I might fix on means of getting over.

Now there seemed little danger in the matter, for our spies had reported no Danes on this side of Parret, for they kept the water between us and them, doubtless knowing that Osric had gone to Brent at first, and thinking it likely that another levy might be made. So the bishop, not very willingly, as it seemed to me, let me go, as there was none else who could go direct to the point as I could without loss of time, even as Osric told him.

Then I gave the standard into Wulfhere's hand, and must seek one to go with me. First I thought of Wislac, but he was a stranger, and then my eyes lit on my collier, and I knew that I need go no further. So I called him, and taking him aside--while the men streamed past us, looking at my silver arms and speaking thereof to one another--told him what we had to do.

Whereat his eyes sparkled, and he said that it was good hearing.

"But, master," he went on, "take off those bright arms of yours and let us go as marshmen. Then will be no suspicion if the Danes see us from across the water."

That was wise counsel, and we left our arms in a baggage wagon, borrowing frocks from the churls who followed us, and only keeping our seaxes in our belts.

Then Dudda found a horse that was led with the wagons, and I bade the man whose it was lend it to him, promising good hire for its use. And so we two rode off together across the marshland, away by Burnham, while the levy held on steadily by the main road.

Then was I glad that I had brought the collier, for the marsh was treacherous and hard to pass in places. But he knew the firm ground, as it were, by nature, and we went on quickly enough. Now and then we passed huts, but they were empty; for away across the wide river mouth at Burnham, though we rode not into that village, we could see the six long black ships as they lay at Stert, and the smoke of the fires their guard had made on shore.

But on this side of the river they had been, for Burnham was but a heap of ashes. They had crossed in their small boats, doubtless, and found the place empty.

Then at last we came to a hut some two miles off in the marshes from Comb-wich, and in that we left our horses, giving them hay from the little rick that stood thereby. To that poor place, at least, the Danes had not come, for the remains of food left on the table showed that the owners had fled hastily, but in panic, and that none had been near the place since.

Now Dudda would have us take poles and a net we found left, on our shoulders, that we might seem fishers daring to return, or maybe driven by hunger to our work. For we must go unhidden soon, where the marshland lay open and bare down to the river, the alder and willow holts ceasing when their roots felt the salt water of the spring tides. But we had been able to keep under their cover as far as the hut.

So we went towards the river, as I had many a time seen the fishers go in the quiet days that were past; and we said little, but kept our eyes strained both up and down the river for sign of the Danes.

But all we saw was once, far off on Stert, the flash of bright arms or helm; and there we knew before that men must be.

On Combwich hill was no smoke wreath of the outpost fires I had feared, nor could I see aught moving among the trees. Then at last we stood on the river bank and looked across at the little haven. All the huts were burnt and silent. There were many crows and ravens among the trees above where they had stood, and a great osprey wheeled over our heads as we looked.

"No men here," said my comrade, "else would not yon birds be so quiet."

But I could see no boat, and my heart sank somewhat; for nothing was there on this bank wherewith to make the raft of which Wulfhere spake.

Then said I: "Let us swim over and see what we can find."

Now it was three hours after noon, or thereabouts, and the tide was running out very swiftly, and it was a long passage over. Nevertheless we agreed to try it, and so, going higher up the stream, we cast ourselves in, and swam quartering across the tide.

A long and heavy swim it was, but no more than two strong men could well manage. All the time, however, I looked to see some red-cloaked Dane come out from the trees and spy us; but there was none.

Then we reached the other bank, and stood to gain breath, for now we were in the enemy's country, and tired as we were, we threw ourselves down in the shelter of a broad-stemmed willow tree, on the side away from the hill and village.

In a moment the collier touched my arm and pointed. On the crest of the hill stood a man, looking down towards us, but he was unarmed, as well as I could see, and, moreover, his figure seemed familiar. We watched him closely, for he began to come down towards us, and as he came nearer I knew him. It was one of the Combwich villeins--a fisher of the name of Elgar.

Now I would speak with him, for he could tell me all I needed; yet I knew not if he had made friends with the Danes, being here and seeming careless.

We lost sight of him among the trees, and the birds flew up, croaking, from them, marking his path as yet towards us; and at last he came from behind a half-burnt hut close to us. Then I called him by name.

He started, and whipped out a long knife, and in a moment was behind the hut wall again. So I knew that he was not in league with the enemy, but feared them. Therefore I rose up and called him again, adding that I was Heregar, and needed him.

Then he came out, staring at me with his knife yet ready. But when he saw that it was really myself he ran to meet me with a cry of joy and knelt before me, kissing my hands and weeping; so that it was a while before I could ask him anything. Very starved and wretched he looked, and I judged rightly that he had taken to the woods from the first.

Presently he was quiet enough to answer my questions, and he told me that at first the Danes had had a strong post on the hill above us; but that, growing confident, they had left it these two days. But there were many passing and repassing along the road, bringing plunder back to the ships. He had watched them from the woods, he said.

Also he told me that even now mounted men had ridden past swiftly, going to the ships, and from that I guessed that Eanulf's force had been seen at least, and tidings sent thereof.

Then I asked him if any boats were left unburnt, and at that a cunning look came into his thin face, and he answered:

"Aye, master. Three of us were minded to save ours, and we sank them with stones in the creek before we fled. But the other two are slain, and I only am left to recover them."

Now that was good hearing, and I bade the men show me where they lay, and going with him found that now the water was low, we could see them and reach them easily. There were two small boats that might hold three men each, and one larger.

Then I told Elgar how I needed them for this night's work, and at first he was terrified, fearing nothing more than that his boats should be lost to him after all. But I promised him full amends if harm came to them, and that in the name of Osric, which he knew well. And with that he was satisfied.

So with a little labour we got the two small boats afloat, and then cast about where to hide them; for though Elgar said that the Danes came not nigh the place, it was likely that patrols would be sent out after the alarm of Eanulf's approach, and might come on them.

At last Elgar said that there was a creek half a mile or less up the river, and on the far side, where they might lie unseen perhaps. And that would suit us well if we could get them there. And the time was drawing on, so that we could make no delay.

Then out of a hollow tree Elgar drew oars for both boats, and we got them out into the river, and Dudda rowing one, and Elgar the other, in which I sat, we went to the place where they should be, keeping under the bank next the Danes. And it was well for us that the tide was so low, for else we should surely have been spied.

Yet we got them into the creek, Elgar making them fast so that they would rise as the water rose. Then he said he would swim back, and if he could manage it would raise the large boat and bring that also.

So without climbing out from under the high banks of the creek he splashed out into the tideway, and started back.

Now Dudda and I must make our way along to the horses, and so we began to get out of the creek, which was very deep, at this low ebb of the water, below the level of the meadows. Dudda was up the bank first, and looked towards Combwich. Then he dropped back suddenly, and bade me creep up warily and look also, through the grass.

So I did, and then knew how near an escape we had had, for there was a party of Danes, idlers as it seemed, among the burnt huts, turning over the ashes with their spears and throwing stones into the water.

Then I saw Elgar's head halfway across the river, and knew he could not see the Danes over the high bank. He was swimming straight for them, and unless he caught sight of one who stood nearest, surely he was lost. It was all that I could do to keep myself from crying out to him; but that would have betrayed us also, and, with us, the hope of our ambush. So we must set our teeth and watch him go.

Then a Dane came to the edge of the high bank and saw him, and at the same moment was himself seen. The Dane shouted, and Elgar stopped paddling with his hands and keeping his head above water.

Now we looked to see him swim back to this bank, and began to wonder if the enemy would follow him and so find us. And for one moment I believe he meant to do so, and then, brave man as he was, gave himself away to save us; for he stretched himself out once more and began to swim leisurely downstream, never looking at the Danes again; for now half a dozen were there and watching him, calling, too, that he should come ashore, as one might guess. But Elgar paid no heed to them, and swam on.

They began to throw stones, and one cast a spear at him, but that fell short. Then the bank hid him from us; but we saw a Dane fixing arrow to bowstring, and saw him shoot; but he missed, surely, for he took another arrow and ran on down the bank.

Then Dudda pulled me by the arm, and motioned me to follow him, and I saw no more.

Now the creek wherein we were ran inland for a quarter mile that we could see, ever bending round so that our boats were hidden from the side where the Danes were. Up that creek we ran, or rather paddled, therefore, knee deep in mud, but quite unseen by any but the great erne that fled over us crying.

Hard work it was, but before the creek ended we had covered half a mile away from danger, and looking back through the grass along the bank could see the Danes no longer. Yet we had no surety that they could not see us, and therefore crawled yet among grass and thistles, along such hollows as we could find.

At last we dared stand up, and still we could see no Danes as we looked back. And then we grew bolder and walked leisurely, as fishers might, not daring to run, across to that hut where the horses were. And reaching that our adventure was ended, for we were safe, and believed ourselves unnoticed if not unseen, for there was no reason why the Danes should think aught of two thralls, as we seemed, crossing the marsh a mile away, and quietly, even if they spied us.

After we reached our horses, there is nothing to tell of our ride back to the bishop. We overtook him before dark, where his men were halted two miles from Bridgwater, on the road, waiting for word from Eanulf.

Much praise gave he to me and the collier for what we had done, as also did Osric. And we, getting our arms again, went back to our own places well content;

eager also was I to tell Wulfhere and Wislac of all that had befallen, and how I had boats for the crossing.

And when they heard how Elgar the fisher had swam on, rather than draw attention to the place where we two lay, Wulfhere nodded and said: "That was well done," and Wislac said: "Truly I would I could do the like of that. Much courage is there in the man who will face a host with comrades beside him against odds; but more is there in the man who will go alone to certain death because thereby he will save others."

Even as we talked there came riding a man from Bridgwater, going fast, yet in no great hurry as it seemed. He rode up to us, for there was the standard, and asked for the bishop, having word from Eanulf for him; and Guthlac told Ealhstan, who came up to speak to him, bidding us bide and listen.

What the man had to tell was this. That the Danes had, in some way, had word of the march of our levies, and had straightway gathered together, or were yet gathering from their raidings here and there, on the steep hill above Bridgwater, having passed through the town, or such as was left thereof after many burnings. And it was Eanulf's plan to attack them there with the first light, if the bishop would join him with his levy.

Then the bishop asked if there had been any fighting. And the man said that there had been some between the van of our force, and the rear of the Danish host; but that neither side had lost many men, nor had there been any advantage gained except to clear the town of the heathen.

Having heard that, Ealhstan bade me go aside with him, and called Osric and some more of the thanes to hold a council. And in the end it was decided that Osric should take on the bulk of the levy to join the ealdorman, while the bishop and I, and two hundred of the men, should try that crossing at Combwich.

"For thus," said Ealhstan, "we can fall on the Danes from behind if they stand or in flank if they retreat."

And except that the bishop would go with me, this pleased them well enough; but they tried to dissuade him from leaving the levy. But he laughed and said that indeed he was only going on before it, for to reach him they would have to go clear through the Danes where they stood thickest, and when they reached the standard, victory would be theirs.

Then they cried that they would surely not fail to reach him, and so the matter was settled, and the thanes told this to their men, who shouted and cheered, so that this seemed to be a good plan after all.

Now the bishop rode among the men, calling out those whom he knew well, and bidding the thanes give him their best, or if they had no best, such as could swim, and very shortly we had full two hundred men ranged on one side of the road, waiting with us, while the rest went off towards Bridgwater, the bishop blessing them ere they started. And as they went they shouted that we should meet again across the ranks of Danes.

When they were gone the bishop bade us rest. And while we lay along the roadside he went up and down, sorting out men who could swim well, and there were more than half who could do so, and more yet who said they were swimmers though poor at it.

Then he told me his plan. How that the men who could not swim must go over first in the boats, and then the arms of the rest should be ferried over while they swam, and so little time would be lost: but all must be done in silence and without lights. So we ate and slept a little, and then, when it grew dark, started off across the meadows. And there the collier guided us well, having taken note of all the ground we had crossed in the morning, as a marshman can.

It was dark, and a white creeping mist was over the open land when we reached it. But over the mists to our left we could see the twinkle of Danish watchfires, where they kept the height over Bridgwater; and again to the right we could see lights of fires at Stert, where the ships lay. But at Combwich were no lights at all, and that was well.

Presently we reached a winding stretch of deep water, and though it was far different when I saw it last, I knew it was the creek in which our boats lay, and up which Dudda and I had fled, full now with the rising tide.

We held on down its course until Dudda told me in a low voice that we were but a bowshot from the boats, and that now it were well for the men to lie down that they might be less easily noticed.

So the word was passed in a whisper down the line, and immediately it seemed as if the force had vanished, as the white mist crept over where they had stood.

Now Dudda and I went down to the boats and there found, not the two we had left only, but a third and larger one beside them. And at first this frightened us, and we stood looking at them, almost expecting armed men to rise from the dark hollows of the boats and fall on us.

Then I would see if such were there, and stepped softly into the nearest. It was empty, and so was the next, and these were our two. Dudda came after me, and he hissed to me under his breath. The oars had been muffled with sacking.

Now none but a friend would have done this, unless it was a most crafty trap to take us withal; and yet to leave the boats as they were had been surer than to meddle with them, if such was meant.

Now Dudda, perplexed as I, though in my heart was a thought that after all Elgar had escaped, stepped into the large boat, and there he started back so suddenly as almost to overturn it, smothering a cry. Then was silence for a moment, while I for my part drew my dagger. Then I saw him stoop down, and again he hissed to me. The boats were afloat, and I drew that I was in up to the big boat.

"Oh, master," said Dudda, whispering, "surely this is Elgar the fisher!"

And I, peering into the dark bottom of the boat could see a dark still form, lying doubled over a thwart, that seemed to me to bear likeness to him.

"Is he dead?" I asked.

"Aye, master, but not long," answered the collier; feeling about.

"Ah!" he said, with a sort of groan, "here is a broken arrow in his shoulder, and in his hand somewhat to muffle the oars withal. Well done, brave Elgar--well done!"

Then I climbed softly over the gunwale, and so it was. Wounded to death as he had been by the arrow shot, he had yet in some way contrived to get this boat here, and afterwards to use his last strength in muffling the oars, and so died, spent, before he could end his task!

And for him I was not ashamed of weeping, thinking there in the darkness, as we bore him hastily to the bank and laid him beyond the reach of hurrying feet to come, of how he must have been shot, and so at once feigning death have floated, or perhaps stranded on the mud, till the Danes were gone, and then returned in spite of pain and growing weakness to do what he had set himself for the sake of his country.

But there was no time for more than thought, and now that we knew the boats safe, I went back to the bishop, and told him that all was ready. And he, ever thoughtful, had told off skilful men to row the boats over, and though now we must have enough for three, he had found six or eight oarsmen, and there was no delay, though they must work with less change, and the tide was still making, so that the pull to Combwich creek would be hard.

Then ten men went softly to the boats, and at the last I bade them pull across to where they might, not making for the creek, and in a minute or two they were gone into the mist and darkness.

Then came crawling to the river bank some six or eight men, strong swimmers, and would have tried to cross; but I bade them wait till the next boatloads went over, so that they might cross beside them, and cling to the gunwale if the stream was too strong. However, though most knew that was good counsel, two must needs try it, and one got across, nearly spent, and the other came back, clinging to the first boat to return, else had he been drowned, and it was a lucky chance that the boat met him.

Now the man who rowed this first boat reported that there was silence, and no sign of Danes, on the other side, and so also did the rest as they came. After that the crossing went on quickly, men swimming beside the boats, and in an hour and a half all were over.

When we found that all was safe, the bishop bade me cross with the standard, and so keep the men together. He himself came last of all.

When Wulfhere came, swimming beside the boat in which sat Wislac, he took three men and went quietly to Combwich, which was nearly half a mile from where we landed, and was back presently, reporting all quiet.

Then Dudda and the other rowers sank the boats, lest they should be seen by chance, and so betray us and our crossing.

Now we went--I leading through this place I knew so well--round the head of the little creek, and so on up the hill, walking in single file almost, and very silently. And when we topped the hill--there before us, among the tree trunks, glowed a little fire, and round that sat six Danes, wrapped in their red cloaks, and, as I could see, all or most of them asleep.

At that I stopped, and the line behind me stopped also, making a clatter of arms as men ran against one another in the dark.

One of the Danes stirred at that, and looked up and round; but he could see nothing, and so folded himself up again. Then I saw that they had an ale cask.

Now I knew that this post must be surrounded and taken, and whispered to Wulfhere, who was next me, what to do. And he answered that he would manage it, bidding me stand still. Then he went down the line, whispering in each man's ear, till he had told off twenty men, and them he sent off right and left into the darkness and I was left with Wislac standing alone, watching the Danes.

I kept my eyes fixed on them till they seemed to waver and grow dim, so intently did I watch them; and then all of a sudden there was the sound of a raven's croak, and into the firelight and on those careless watchers leapt Wulfhere and his men from all around.

There was one choked cry, and that was all, and Wulfhere beckoned to me. I advanced, and the line closed up and followed.

Now we stood on Combwich hill, and all was well so far. Ealhstan came up to me, unknowing of what had caused the halt, being over the brow of the hill, and when he knew, said it was well done, and that now we might rest safely for a time.

So we bade the men sit down, and those who were wet made up the fire afresh: for there was no need to put it out, but rather reason for allowing the Danes to see it burning, as if in safety.

When we three sat by the bishop, Wislac asked what we were to wait for, and, indeed, that must be the next thought.

Then said the bishop that after a while he would take the force to the woods that overhung the roadway, and so wait for the Danes as Eanulf and Osric drove them back; but that it was not more than midnight yet.

Then came a little silence, and in that I seemed to hear the sound of footsteps coming up the hill from Combwich, and bade the others listen. And at the same time some of the men heard the sound, and started up to see who came. But they were the steps of one man only, walking carelessly.

Into the light of the fire stepped one, at the sight of whom the men stared, though Wislac laughed quietly. It was that young thane who had wanted to fight my friend Wislac on the day of the council. He was very wet, and tired, throwing himself down beside us when he saw where we sat.

Ealhstan asked him who bade him come, and how he had followed us.

"Nearly had I forgotten a dispute I have with Wislac the Thane here. Wherefore I asked no man's leave, but followed you just too late for the crossing. So needs must swim. And here am I to see that Wislac counts fairly, and that he may have the same surety of me."

Whereat we were obliged to laugh, and most of all the bishop, because he would fain have been angry, and could not. Then the thane, whose name was Aldhelm, asked who was the slain man over whose body he had well-nigh fallen on the other side of the river. So I told them of Elgar the fisher and of his brave deeds, and they were silent, thinking of what his worth was; too great indeed for praise. Only the bishop said he should surely have a mound raised over him as over a warrior, charging us three, or whichever lived after this fight, to see to that.

Now we slept a little, posting sentries at many points, and giving those next the Danes on either side the red cloaks of the picket we had slain, lest daylight should betray them. It was in all our minds that at daybreak our men would attack from Bridgwater, driving the Danes back on us, and so we should fall on them while they were retreating, and complete the victory. So we had men on the hill overlooking the road to Bridgwater through Cannington that they might give us the first warning.

Therefore I slept quietly, and all with me. And as I slept I dreamed.

It seemed that I was standing alone on Brent Hill and from that I could look all over the land of Somerset, as an eagle might look, but being close to everything that I would see. And I saw all that I had done since I stood there as a prisoner, watching myself curiously in all that I did, and yet knowing all the thoughts that drove me to deed after deed.

And so through the mirk wood till I turned and slew, and armed myself, and tormented my prisoner; then to the collier's hut, and my talking with the child; then on till I saw the lights of the viking ships and so thereafter bore the war arrow-
-everything, till at last I saw myself sleeping under the trees, on the top of this hill of Combwich, and there I thought my dream would surely end; but it did not.

For now out of the shadows came Matelgar and stood beside me and waked me, and he told me that when the tide was out I must be up and doing. And so he passed. And the old crone, Gundred, came out of the shadows, and sat on her bundle of sticks and looked at me, and she too bade me be up and doing when the tide was low. And she looked at the standard that lay beside me, and said, "Aye, a standard; but not yet the Dragon of Wessex"; and so she, too, faded away.

And then came Alswythe, and as she came, it seemed, as I looked, that I stretched my arms to her; but she smiled and said, "Love, when the tide is out, I shall be praying in the abbey for you and your men."

And then from beside her came Turkil, the little child, smiling also, but hanging to Alswythe's dress as he said, "Warrior, when the water falls low, my father will call me from the hill, and I will pray for you and for him."

So these two were gone. And at that I seemed to see our men lie in Bridgwater, and there was Turkil's father, the franklin, sleeping with the rest. But up and down among them went Eanulf the Ealdorman, watching ever.

Then fled I, as it were, to that hill where lay the Danes, and on the road thither I saw Osric and twenty men, looking up at the fires that burnt where the enemy lay.

And then I looked on those fires, and there were no men round them.

One shook me by the shoulder, and my dream went.

It was Dudda, and his eyes were bright in the firelight.

And over Brent the first streaks of dawn were broadening, and the mists were gone.

"Master, master," he said, "come with me to the roadway. Something is afoot."

Then I woke Wulfhere, asking him to wait for me, guarding the standard, and followed my man swiftly to the place where the road cuts the hill. And there was a knot of the men, standing and listening.

I listened also, and far off towards Cannington I could hear the sound of the tread of many feet, for the morning was still and quiet; and the men said that this was growing nearer.

Then knew I that the Danes were falling back to the ships without risking battle, and my dream came back to me, with its vision of unguarded watch fires, and it seemed to me that surely, unless we could stay them, they would depart with the tide as it fell.

"How is the tide?" asked I of the men round me.

"Failing now," said one who knew, "but not fast."

Then I remembered things I had hardly noted in years gone by. How the tide hung around Stert Point, as though Severn and Parret warred for a while, before the mighty Severn ebb sucked Parret dry, and how the ebb at last came swift and sudden.

"When the tide is low," said they whom I had seen in my dream.

And in a moment I recalled the first fight, and the words of Gundred, and I knew that we had the Danes in a trap.

They were marching now in time to gain their ships and be off as the last man stepped on board, with the full draft of the ebb to set them out to sea beyond Lundy Isle, into open water. Nor had they left their post till the last moment, lest our levy should be on their heels, or else some more distant marauding party had not come in till late.

I went back to Wulfhere and told him this, and in it all he agreed.

And, as we whispered together, Ealhstan sat up, asking quickly, "Who spoke to me?" and looking round for one near him, as it seemed.

"None spoke, Father," said I, "or none but Wulfhere to me, whispering."

"What said Wulfhere?"

"That the tide was failing," I answered.

The bishop was silent for a moment, and then he said:

"I heard a voice, plainly, that cried to me, 'Up! for the Lord has delivered these heathen into your hands'."

"We heard no such voice, Father," I said, "but I think it spoke true."

Now the light was broadening, making all things cold and gray as it came. And quickly I told Ealhstan what I had heard, and what both I and Wulfhere thought of the matter.

"Can we let them pass us, and so fall on them as they gain the level land of Stert?" asked Ealhstan, saying nothing more.

"That can we," I answered. "They will keep to the road, and we can draw back to the edge of the hill, so taking them in flank as they leave it."

For the hills bend round a little beyond the place where the road falls into the level below Matelgar's hall.

"So be it," said the bishop. "Go you, Wulfhere, and see how near the host is, and come back quickly."

When he was gone the bishop bade me wake the men. And at first I was for going round, but by this thane Wislac had waked, and had been listening to us: and he said that if I would let him wake the men he could do it without alarm or undue noise. Only I must raise the standard and bid them be silent. At that the bishop smiled and nodded, and I raised the standard, and waited.

Then Wislac stood up and crowed like a cock, and instantly the men began to turn and sit up, and as their eyes lit on the standard raised in their midst, became broad awake, each man rousing the next sleeper if one lay near him. And there was the bishop, finger on lip, and they were silent.

"Verily I thought on the hard chapel stones," muttered Guthlac, the lay brother, behind me.

"It is the war chime, not the matin bell, you shall hear this morning," said one of his brethren.

"That is better--mea culpa," said Guthlac, clapping his hand on his mouth to stop his own warlike ejaculation.

Then came Wulfhere back, swiftly. Barely a mile were they from the hill, he said, and coming on quickly in loose order. Moreover, a horseman had passed, riding hard to the ships, doubtless to bid them be ready. But that would take little time, for these vikings are ever ready for flight, keeping their ships prepared from day to day.

CHAPTER XV. THE GREAT FIGHT AT PARRET MOUTH.

Now very silently we drew off from that place to the edge of the hill which looks across the road to Stert. And there the bishop drew us up in line, four deep, and told the men what we must do, bidding them be silent till we charged, though that could not prevent a hum of stern approval going down the line.

One man the bishop called out by name, and when he stood before him, bade him, as a swift runner, hasten back to Eanulf or Osric, and bid them on here with all speed. And, when the man's face fell, the bishop bade him cheer up and go, for the swifter he went the sooner would he be back at the sword play. Whereat the man bowed, and, leaving his mail at a tree foot, started at a steady run over the ground we had covered already, and was lost in the trees.

Then we waited, and the light grew stronger every moment. As we lay in line among the bushes we could see without much fear of being ourselves seen, and by and by we could make out the ships. They had their masts raised, and the sails were plain to be seen, ready for hoisting. The men were busy about their decks, and on shore as well, while the vessels were yet close up to the land.

They must haul off soon, little by little, or they would be aground, as doubtless they had been with every tide till this, for rocks are none, only soft mud on which a ship may lie safely, but through which no man may go, save on such a "horse" as the fishers use to reach their nets withal, sledge-like contrivances of flat boards which sink not.

The wait seemed long, but at last we heard the hum of voices, and the tramp of feet, and our hearts beat fast and thick, for the time was coming.

Over the hill and down it they streamed in a long, loose line, laughing and shouting as the ships came in sight. A long breath came from us, and there was a little stir among the men; but the time was not yet, and we crouched low, waiting to make our spring.

Then ran up a long red forked flag, with a black raven on it, from the largest ship, and that seemed to be a signal for haste, for the tide was failing, so that some of the foremost men began to stream away from their comrades. And then I saw that many carried packs full of plunder, and also that the last of them were on the level.

So also saw the bishop, and he rose to his feet, pointing with the great mace he bore (for he might not wield sword) to the Danes, and saying:

"For the honour of Dorset--for the holy cross--charge!"

With a mighty shout we rose up, each in his place, and down the hill we rushed sword and axe aloft, on that straggling line.

Then from the Danes came a howl of wrath and terror, and, for a moment, dropping their burdens, they fled in a panic towards the ships.

Yet that was not the way of Danish men and vikings, and that flight stayed almost before it had gone fifty yards. Up rose amidst the throng a mighty double axe, and a great voice was heard shouting, and round their chief began to form a great ring of tried warriors, shoulder to shoulder as well as might be. But that ring might not be perfect all at once--too close were we upon them, having already cut down many of the last to fly.

And then the battle began in earnest, and I will tell what I saw of it. For I was in the centre of our line, as befitted, and on either side of me were Wulfhere and Wislac, and on either side of them again, my collier next to Wulfhere, and next to Wislac his young thane. Before me were Guthlac and two brethren, and the other three behind me. That was the standard's shield wall. Behind that came Ealhstan the Bishop, hemmed in by twelve of his own best men.

So, with voice, and gesture of arm and mace the bishop swung our line in a half circle round the face of that grim ring of vikings, and as they closed up we closed, and faced them. Then saw I that we were outnumbered by three to one, but we were fresh, and they tired with a long march, quickly made, and under burdens.

Now began the spears to fly from one side to the other, and men began to fall. And yet there was no great attack made on either side. Then grew I impatient, for it seemed to me that as we were the weaker side the first charge might do all for us. So I spoke to Wulfhere, saying:

"We must charge before they. Let us break into that circle."

"Aye!" said the veteran, and "Aye!" shouted Wislac; and so I pointed the banner forward and shouted for my shield men to charge.

And that, with a great roar, they did; and down before the brawny arms of those foremost three lay brethren went three of the heathen, and we were pressing into the circle. Then a brother fell, dragging a Dane with him, and Wislac took his place, and three more Danes fell. Then went Aldhelm to Wislac's side, and Lo! the circle was broken, and our standard stood in the midst.

Yet was not that ring destroyed, and in a moment it closed after us, and now were we ten in the midst of a crowd of foes, while again outside them raged Ealhstan and his men, striving to break through to us.

Then knew I that our case was hard, and I struck the spear that held the standard into the ground, and round it we stood, back to back, Wulfhere and Wislac once more to right and left of me. And it would seem that so grim looked we in our desperation, that they feared us a little, or, at least, that each feared to be the first to fall on us, for the Danes drew back and let us stand for a breathing space, until that great chief who rallied the men--leaving the care of the outer ring for a moment --came and faced me, speaking in fair Saxon enough, and bidding us surrender.

And for answer I threw my seax at him, and as he raised shield to stop it, for it flew straight and hard as a forester can throw, I leapt at him, going in under his shield, and he fell heavily, moving not, for my blow went home. Well it was that Wulfhere came after me, for he warded blow of axe that would have slain me. And then the Danes howled and fell on us.

Hard fighting it was, but round us grew a ring of dead, and no man had laid hands on the standard. Guthlac was down, and Aldhelm, two lay brethren also, and we were all but sped when I was ware of a Saxon shout, and the crash of a great mace on a helmet before me, and then, "Well done, my sons!" cried Ealhstan the Bishop, as he came and ringed us round with his own men, and we might breathe again.

Now was the ring of Danes parted, and the ring was of our men; yet round it raged the vikings, as we had raged round their ring but a short space before. Yet, every man of us knew that we had won, for, even if each one of us fell before Eanulf came, the ships would not sail that tide. For the tall masts were listing over as two ships took the ground unheeded, and four were hauling out as the tide fell.

And I thought of my vision last night, and of those I had seen, and of what they had bid me think of them; and the roar of battle went on unheeded by me as I leant against the standard staff while I might, and found my strength again.

"See," cried Wislac, pointing. And I looked over to the hill where the road came down. It was full of horsemen, charging with levelled spears, and surely that was Osric at their head! Then near me a voice cried thrice "Victory!" but it seemed not as one of our men's rough voices, but very strange.

Over the level the spearmen swept, and a cry broke from the Danes as they saw the fresh foe upon them, and again they fell back from us quickly, and, spite of our charge on them, and the spears of the leading horsemen, once more closed up into their iron ring. But now it was not motionless, but moved ever towards the ships, going backward steadily.

Round it went Osric and his men: but into it they could not break. For the Danes hewed the ash shafts of the spears, and near them no horse might live, for their axes would shear through man and horse alike.

Then Ealhstan shouted to Osric, bidding us stand. And right glad were we to do this, while ever the Danes shrank away from us.

"Trapped they are, Sheriff," said Ealhstan, when Osric rode up to him, bearing still a headless spear. "Let them bide till Eanulf comes. None can reach the ships."

"He is hard behind me with all the levy," said Osric. "Let us finish this without him."

But Ealhstan shook his head, pointing to our men. And when he looked more coolly, he saw that barely half of us were left, and those worn out. So must we stand and wait; but we had done what we went to do, and had trapped the heathen when the tide was low. Yet the Danes went steadily back towards their ships, having yet half a mile to cover, but they left a line of wounded men to mark where they had gone, as one after another dropped.

Now were we who were left safe, and knew we had done a deed which would he told and sung till other tales of victory blotted out its remembrance if they might.

Then Ealhstan bade us sit down, for our horsemen were between us and the foe, and thereon he raised his voice, and with one accord his lay brethren and his own housecarles joined in singing a psalm of victory. And it was just at the matin time--yet that psalm ended not as it was wont, for ere the last verses were sung, it was drowned in a great and thundering war song of Wessex, old as the days of Ceawlin or beyond him. And if I mistake not, in that song bishop and lay brethren joined, leaving the chant for their own native and well-loved tongue, else would they have been the only men of all the host unstirred thereby and silent.

Now, from that war song came a strange thing. It caused two great Danes to go berserk in their rage, and back they flew on us, their shields cast aside, and their broad axes overhead, howling and foaming as they came.

One of Osric's men tried to stop them. But he and his horse fell, for (I say truth) one leapt high above the horse, smiting downwards with his axe, so that the man was swept in twain under that blow, and the berserk Dane came on unhindered, straight for the standard, for his comrade had hewed off the horse's head.

Now I rested, by the standard, a long spear's length in front of our line. But by this I had leapt to my feet; and it was time, for he was almost on me. Spear had I none; so I dragged out the standard shaft from the ground where I had struck it, and levelled that sharp butt end full at his chest. Overhead was his axe again, and I had no shield to stop the blow; but I must leap aside from it.

He paid no heed to the spear-ended shaft, but rushed straight on it, spitting himself through and through, while his axe fell; but I had wrenched myself and the shaft at once to one side, and he fell over, burying the axe head in the ground but an inch from the collier's foot. Yet had he not done with me, for, leaving the axe, he clawed the ashen shaft and dragged himself up along it, howling, not with the pain, but with madness, and I must needs smite him with my sword, for his dagger was already at my throat.

Then looked I round for the other, but at first could not see him, for he was dead also, pinned to the ground by another of the horsemen, from behind. And all our men were on their feet, and the ring of Danes were shouting, and cheering their two mad men, yet keeping close order.

This seems long in telling; but it was all done in a flash, as it were, for the first I knew of the coming of these men was by the wheeling of the horse and the leaping of the berserk above it.

Then my men came and rid the standard of its burden, not easily, while Ealhstan stood with his arm on my shoulder, looking white and scared: for that had been the greatest danger he had seen that day, as he told me, which, indeed, it must have been, for else he had never changed countenance.

"Gratias Domino," he said, "verily into these heathen evil spirits enter, driving them to death. Now have you fought the evil one, both spiritually and bodily, my son, and have won the victory!"

Even as he spoke, the men, being sure of no more of such comings, began to crowd round me, shouting and cheering as though I had done some great deed. Which, if it were such, it seems to me that great deeds are forced on men at times; for what else I could have done I know not, unless, as Wislac says, I had run away, even as he was minded to do. But I had no time for that, nor do I believe his saying concerning himself.

When the Danes were nigh their ships Ealhstan bade us tend our wounded. And the first man tended was myself, for Wulfhere came to me, looking me over, and at last binding a wound on my left shoulder, of which I knew not, saying that my good mail had surely saved me. He himself had a gash across his face, and Wislac one on the leg, but none of us was much hurt.

Then Wislac sought Aldhelm, whom he found sitting up, dazed, from a blow across the helm that had stunned him, but he was soon able to walk, though dizzy and sick. But Guthlac was slain outright, and two others of the brethren.

Well, so might I go on, for of all our two hundred men there were left but ninety fit to go on with the fight, the rest being slain or sore wounded by the Danish axes. Ealhstan was unhurt; for, save that once when he had broken the ring to reach us when we were hemmed in, his men had kept before him.

Now what befell after that will not bear telling; for it was not long before Eanulf and all the Somerset and the rest of the Dorset levy came down and fell on the Danes as they fought their last fight as brave men should, with a quarter mile of deep mud between them and their ships.

Into that fight none of us bishop's men went, for we had done our part. But we lay and saw the Danes charge again and again against odds, their line growing thinner each time, until our men swept the last of them from the bank into the ooze, and there was an end.

Yet a few managed, I know not how, to reach the ships, and there they were safe; but thence they constantly shot their arrows into our men, harmless enough, but yet showing their mettle.

So was a full end made of that host, for none but those few were left alive from Stert field, and Somerset and Dorset had taken their fill of vengeance.

But, for all the victory, down sat Ealhstan the Bishop, and hiding his face in his hands wept that such things could be, and must be till war is no more.

CHAPTER XVI. AT GLASTONBURY.

On that hard-won field we lay all that day, for we knew not if more Danes were left up country, or if by chance the ships might fall into our hands with the rising tide. And I think we might have taken them had not our men, in their fury, broken the boats which lay along the bank; so that we could not put off to them. Therefore, as the tide rose again and they floated, the men on board hauled out, and setting sail with much labour, for there were very few in each ship, stood off into mid channel. Out of Severn they could not get, for the wind was westerly, and the tide setting eastward, so at last they brought up in the lee of the two holms, and there furled sail and lay at anchor.

Very stiff and sore were we when we had rested for a little, and there fell a sadness on the levy, now that the joy of battle had gone, and the cost of victory must be counted. And that was heavy, for so manfully and steadily had the vikings fought that they had accounted for man to man as nearly as one might count, either slain or maimed.

Now on this matter I heard Wislac speak to Aldhelm, who sat facing him, and holding his aching head with both hands.

"So, friend," quoth Wislac, "as touching that matter of dispute we had. How stands the account?"

"I know not, nor care," said Aldhelm. "All I wot is that my head is like to split."

"Nay, that will it not, having stood such a stout blow," said Wislac, laughing. "Cheer up, and count our score of heads."

"I can count but one head, and that my own. Let it bide."

"So, that is better," said Wislac. "I should surely have been slain five times by my own count, but it seems I am wrong. Wherefore I must have escaped somehow. And that is all I know about it."

Then he turned to me, and asked if I had noted any doings at all.

And when I thought, all I could remember plainly were the fall of the tall chief I slew, and the coming of Ealhstan, and the attack of the berserk, and no more; all the rest was confused, and like a dream. So I said that it seemed to me that we had had no time to do more than mind ourselves, but that withal my shield wall had kept the standard. And that kept, there need be no question as to who had done best.

Then Wislac nodded, after his wont, and said that if Aldhelm was content so was he.

Whereupon Aldhelm held out his hand, and said that Wislac was wise and he foolish. And Wislac, grasping it, answered that it was a lucky foolishness that had brought so stout a comrade to his side, for had it not been for Aldhelm putting his thick head betwixt him and an axe, slain he would have been.

"Aye, brother," he said, "deny it not, for I saw you thrust yourself forward and save me by yourself, which doubtless is your way of settling a grudge, brother, and a good one."

So those two were sworn friends from that day forward, as were many another couple who met on that field for the first time, fighting side by side for Wessex.

Thus wore away the day and the next night, and with the morning those ships were yet under the holms, swinging at their anchors, for the westerly breeze held.

Then said Eanulf: "Let them be; harm can they do none, being so few. They will go with the shift of wind."

But the shift of wind came not for days and days, and there they lay, never putting out from shelter. And they are out of my story, so that I will say what befell them.

One night it freshened up to a gale, and in the morning there were five ships where six had been. One had sunk at her moorings. Then men said that the Danes had made a hut on the flat holm, plain to be seen from the nearest shore. And at last a shift of wind came, and they put not out.

So certain fishers dared to sail across and spy what was amiss, and finding no man in the ships, nor seeing any about the hut, went ashore, none hindering them.

Ships and hut and shore were but the resting place of the dead, for after a while they had no food left, and were too few and weak even to man one ship and go.

Many a long year it was before the king of their land, Norse or Dane, whichever he was, learned what had befallen his host, and how their bones lay on the Wessex shore and islands, for not one of all that had sailed that spring returned to give the news, or to tell how his comrades died on Stert fighting to the last, and on the island wishing they had fallen with the slain.

Now must I tell how we went back to Glastonbury town, marching proudly as became conquerors, while on every side was shouting of men, and at the same time weeping of women for those who had fallen.

When we came to the great square there stood Tatwine the Abbot and all his monks; but I had no eyes for them. For there, with abbess and nuns, stood Alswythe, smiling on me through tears of joy, and though her cheeks were thinner and paler by reason of fasting and prayer for us all, looking most beautiful, and to me like a vision of some saint.

That was all I could see of her then, for we must kneel, while a great Te Deum was sung, and then crowd into the abbey to hear mass once more.

Then after that was over, there was a great feast in the wide hall of the abbey, where Ealhstan and Eanulf sat side by side in the high seats, and on their right, Osric and myself, and on the left, Wulfhere and Wislac, none grudging those chief places to the men who had kept the standard and broken the Danish ring.

When the feasting was done, then came the telling of great deeds over the ale cup, and that lasted long, and many were the brave men praised; nor were the deeds of the vikings, as brave foes, forgotten, for men praised them also. Moreover, the gleemen sang of the fight, and in those songs my name came so often, as needs it must, seeing that I bore the standard, that I will not set them down. Nor is there need, for the housecarles sing them even yet.

Now before we went to rest, Eanulf bade me wait on him early in the morning, and so, being refreshed by a long, quiet night, I went to him as he had bidden me.

There he thanked me as man to man for that crossing of Parret, and for staying the going of the Danes, saying that a greater man than he should add to the thanks. For needs must that one took word of all that had befallen to Ethelwulf the King, and that to be such a messenger was most honourable. Therefore should I myself bear the news, taking with me my two friends and such men as I chose, and should bear, written down, the reports of both Osric and Ealhstan, besides his own.

"Else," said he, "there are perhaps some to whom credit is due whose names may pass unmentioned."

And thanking him, I said that that was likely, for I knew few in the levy, which came from far and wide.

Whereat he laughed, saying that I was either very modest or very simple. So I knew that he spoke of myself, and thanked him again.

"Nay," he said, "small thanks to me, for if I did you not justice the men would."

Then all of a sudden he asked me about the business of my trial, and what I thought of it, bidding me tell him as a friend, thinking naught of the judge.

And that I was able to do now without passion, so far off and small a thing it seemed after all these stirring doings. And I knew that but for it I had been only a foolish thane, and slain maybe over my feasting in my own hall, or on Combwich hill, with my back to the foe, beside Matelgar.

Now when I had ended my tale and my thoughts concerning it, he told me that he had found out much of late, as he and the thanes spoke together here while waiting for the levy, and that word should go to the king of the whole matter, so that without waiting for the Moot, he should inlaw me again.

Then I knew not enough to say; but he clapped me on the shoulder, saying that he had been an unjust judge for once, and that I must be heedful if ever I sat in his place, and so bid me go and find my friends--and get ready to ride to Salisbury, where the king lay, having moved from Winchester nearer to us.

That went I to do with a light heart, and only sorry that I might not see Alswythe before I went.

And this I told Wislac, who looked oddly at me, and then laughed, saying that he believed I feared an old nun more than a wild berserk. And true it was that I was afraid of that stately abbess, though not in the same way as one fears a raging madman flying on one.

"Pluck up courage," said he, "and go and ask the old dame to let you have speech with your lady; and if she grants it not, I am mistaken, for the lady is not one of her nuns, and there is a guest chamber for such folk as bishop's right-hand men, surely!"

That was good counsel, and so I went to the nunnery, trembling first because I was afraid, and next lest I might not see Alswythe.

Now that wondrous silver mail of mine was too easily known, and so soon as I got out into the street, the beggar men began to shout and crawl towards me. And then others looked, and ran, and then more, till there was a crowd of men of the levy pressing round me, stretching hands to pat me and the like.

Then one stood in front of me, hands on hips, and stared at me, and all at once he shouted: "Ho, comrades, this is the saint of Cannington hill! I saw him there, and soundly did he rate me for running, even as I deserved."

And at that there was a mighty shouting and crowding, so that I could in no wise go on my way, and I began to wax wroth.

My back was to the abbey gates, which were closed after me by the porter, and just then I saw some of the men look up over my head and point, and laugh; so I turned round, and there were Eanulf and Osric on the gateway battlements, looking on, as drawn thither by the noise. And just then Eanulf, laughing, made some sign or speech which I could not hear, to the men, who cheered; and soon they brought a great shield and on that set me, in spite of myself, raising me up shoulder high and saluting me as the man who had gained all the honour and victory. There must I lie still, lest I should fall and be made to look more foolish yet, and when I sat up, crosslegged thereon, they stopped shouting and stared at me.

"Let me down, ye pigs!" said I, very cross, and unmindful of the honour they would do me.

"Speak to us, Thane; speak to us," they cried; and one--he who knew me at Cannington after the first fight--added:

"Aye, Thane, you made us strong again on the hill the other day-- blaming us rightly. Praise us now if that may be."

Then I cast about for what to say, not being a great hand at speaking, though maybe, when real occasion is, the words have come fast enough. Howbeit, this was in coolness. But I knew that they were worthy of praise, so I said:

"Well have ye done, every man of you, even as I knew ye would when once ye turned to bay. And if the Danes come again, as I think they will not speedily, fight as ye fought at Stert, and there will be victory again."

Then they cheered and shouted again, louder than before; and I made to leap down, but they would not suffer me.

Then said I: "Let me go, for I have an errand."

Whereupon the men who held the shield, and could hear me amid the slackening uproar, asked where I would go, and being dazed by the noise and tumult, like an owl in daylight, I must needs answer, without thinking; "To the great nunnery."

And the end of that foolishness was that they bore me thither, for it was not far, with a great crowd of all sorts following and shouting. And there must I stand with all that tail after me while they beat on the gates in such sort that the poor nuns must have thought the Danes at their doorstep.

But I held up my hand for silence, not thinking it would come; but as it were by nature longing for it. And instantly all the crowd was hushed, and that surprised me, though when I told Wulfhere thereof he said it was no wonder.

Seeing which I begged them all to go away and not scare the holy women, who were used to quiet in the place. And then I remembered the honour the honest warriors had meant this for, and thanked them, bidding them make allowances for my being put out at first.

Then took they off their helms and shouted thrice; and then fled rapidly, for the gates opened behind me, and there was the abbess herself, with her cheeks red, and her eyes burning bright in anger, as I thought, while behind her peeped all her nuns at the crowded street, and at myself standing shamefaced on the steps, doffing my helm as I saw her.

But instead of being angry, she held out both her hands, and spoke kindly, saying; "Never has our quiet place heard such clamour before; but we women will not be behind the men in welcoming Heregar;" and so she bade the nuns come forward, laying her hands on my shoulder, and adding; "See, daughters, this is he who dared to warn the land of its danger, saving the lives of our sisters of Bridgwater, and many others, and who has even now led the host and conquered, giving us safety and peaceful rest again."

But I knelt and kissed her hand, while there went a little murmur among the nuns.

Then the lady abbess touched gently my bound shoulder, and said that the hurt was but rudely tended and that she must bind it afresh; so should she show her gratitude to one who had bled for the land. And they led me into the courtyard; and thence to the guest chamber, and there waited Alswythe.

Now when I looked to see her greet me formally, as in the presence of the abbess, she ran into my arms, and I found that we were alone.

Then must she hear and I tell all that had happened to me since we parted; but that was too long for the telling then, for very soon the abbess came with clatter of vessels along the passage, bringing warm water and salves to bind my small wound afresh.

And in that Alswythe helped her, with many pitying words and soft touches, so that I thought it good to be hurt if such tendance might ever be had. And many things they asked, as of Wulfhere's safety, and the collier's, and of how I got that wound, and the like. And that last I could not tell them, marvelling myself when it came, and more that it was the only one; but I know I smote flatwise once or twice myself in the heat of fight, so doubtless it was so with others, else would Aldhelm have been in halves or thereabouts.

Then I told them of my message to the king, and at that Alswythe rejoiced. And the abbess said that doubtless the king would reward the messenger, and what reward would I ask an he did so?

Now there was only one reward to me in all the world, and for answer I took Alswythe's hand, all wet with the water she bathed my hurt with, and kissed it. On which the maiden blushed, and looked down, but the abbess laughed softly, saying, "Verily, I thought so," and then seemed to choke a little, turning away from us. And Alswythe did not draw away her hand from mine, but let her cheek rest for a moment against my head, and so there was a little silence.

Then the abbess turned round again, and her eyes were bright, but the shine was of tears in them, and she spoke briskly.

"Now must you get hence, Heregar, my son, and go your way to the king with all haste, so shall you be back the sooner. Give him a scarf to bind that wound, Alswythe; so shall it seem an honour and not a scar."

So there was a little leave taking, but not much, though enough, and I went from the nunnery with Alswythe's white and red and gold scarf over my shoulder; gay enough to look at, but no gayer than the heart beneath it.

And there, waiting for me in the street, was my tail, armed and drawn up in line of fours to see me back to the abbey. So I went there at the head of them, with more shouting of people.

There was Wulfhere sitting on the doorsteps of the great door, having a bag in his hand, and when I got up to him, he thrust it out to me, saying "largess", and that I was glad enough to understand.

So I put my hand into the bag, and crying, "Here is withal to drink to Somerset and Dorset shoulder to shoulder," scattered the silver pennies among them, and so left them without any order among them at all, though shoulder to shoulder certainly.

"Ho, master!" said Wulfhere, "you looked mighty angry when you were carried aloft an hour ago."

"Aye," said I, "'tis pity a thane cannot walk abroad quietly on his own business."

"Well, well, they thought that you were their business, doubtless."

"Whence came all those pennies?" I asked, for we had no store at all to cast away.

"From Eanulf and Ealhstan," said Wulfhere, laughing. "They came to me, and saying that they were sore jealous, and minded to have good cause therefor, gave me this that you might carry off all well to the end."

And that was good of them, for else I know not how I should have left the men without more speech making.

Just then came the ealdorman into the hall where we were, and laughing, asked me if I meant to take all that following to Salisbury. But I only wanted the standard guards who were left, and Aldhelm, as one who had fought as such. This I had told Wulfhere before, so that I was not surprised when I heard that all were ready, and but waiting for me to set off.

Then Eanulf and Osric took me to the bishop, and there gave me writings to deliver to the king, and also bade me tell all that he asked, in my own way.

And those three saw us set forth, all well mounted, and a goodly company to look at, the bishop blessing us before we went, and the people and warriors following and cheering us on our way through the town, and even some way beyond the walls.

CHAPTER XVII. ALFRED THE ATHELING.

Of our long ride to the king's place there is little to tell. Only that everywhere the news seemed to have flown before us, and men knew who we were and what our errand, crowding round us to hear all about the fighting, and to be assured that the Danes had truly gone. And great cheer made they for us everywhere, so that we were treated as princes almost.

Therefore, that was a merry ride and a pleasant in the early June weather, and we were ever cheerful, for it so happened, as may have been already seen, that no one of us had lost close friend or kin in the battles, but had the rather gained much. Yet maybe we were the only ones of whom that might be said; for mixed with the joy was mourning over all the land. And of all my company, I had the most cause to be lighthearted; so that for all I had gained I thought the hard things I had gone through were well worth the bearing. Ever, therefore, have I judged him the happiest who out of hardship gains rest; for he best knows its worth.

So at last we came to Salisbury town, and that was full of a brilliant company: the courtiers of the king, and their following again. Yet, for all their magnificence, thanks to our good bishop's gifts, we showed well as we rode into the streets, and I think were envied by many because the marks of honourable war were yet on us; so that the men spoke of Aldhelm's crushed headpiece, or Wulfhere's gashed shield that bore the mark of the axe that he stopped from me, or my riven mail that Alswythe's scarf would scarcely hide, and Wislac's broken crest.

And if they looked from us to our men, there was yet more of the like to speak about; for not one of the standard guard had been scatheless from heavy weapon play.

Being thus marked we were easy to be known, and hardly had we drawn rein at the great hostelry where we should wait till the king summoned us, when a thane came to me, asking if we were from bishop or ealdorman. And when I said we were so, bearing letters from them, he bade us to the king's presence at once, tarrying for nothing, as we were waited for.

Fain would we have washed away the stains of travel; but he was urgent, saying that the king's word brooked no delay. Therefore, leaving our horses with the people of the inn, we followed him, marching in order, to the great house where Ethelwulf was.

Here were guards and many thanes, and I must show the tokens given me, before we might enter, while our thane stood by, impatient at the formalities.

Those over, we came to a greet hall high-ceiled with oak, and carved everywhere, and strewn with sweet sedges, and on the high place sat the king and queen and one of the athelings.

Now I had never seen the king before, but I thought him like all that I had heard of in stories. For he sat in his purple robes, ermine-trimmed, having on a little gold crown over his long, curling hair, and his gloves and shoes were of cloth of gold, curiously wrought with pearls, while at his feet sat a page, holding a cushion whereon lay sceptre and orb.

But I looked to see the face of a warrior under the gold circle of the king, and therein was disappointed; for his face was kind and gentle, as many a good warrior's has been in time of peace, but lacked those lines which a man might know would harden into grimness and strength in time of need. And I thought that Ealhstan was like a king, and Ethelwulf like a bishop rather.

Yet by the king's side, leaning on his chair, was one whom I then noted not, having eyes only for his father--Alfred the Atheling, who, to my mind, is both warrior and saint, as though Ethelwulf, his father, and Ealhstan, his teacher, had each taught him the properties of the other, making a perfect king.

Now, while I looked, our guide went and made obeisance before the king, telling him of our coming, and at that the face of Ethelwulf lighted up, and he called to us to come near and give our message. And I saw the queen clasp her hands, as preparing to hear things all too heavy for a lady's ear, while the atheling stood up and gazed eagerly at us. Then, too, over all the court was deep silence, as they made a lane through which we must pass to reach the throne, and our feet seemed to make all the sound there was.

So we tramped up, and bowed low before the king, who ran his eyes over us, though not as a captain: but as one who knows men of all sorts well, and is accustomed to judge their faces.

Then he said to me; "You are Heregar, the bishop's standard bearer. We have heard of you as such, and welcome you, knowing you must bring good news, as your face tells me."

"I am Heregar, Lord King," I answered, "and I bring good news--written in these which I am to give into your own hand."

Then the king smiled a little, and signed the atheling to take the letters, and give them him.

But I, not knowing court ways, must needs think this beside my duty, and said quickly, not knowing to whom I spoke; "Pardon me, Thane, I am to give these into the king's own hand," and so stepped past him, holding out the letters to Ethelwulf.

And at that the atheling laughed outright, which was strange to me in the king's presence, saying, "Not so far wrong, standard bearer, if not very polite;" and so stepped back to his place, still laughing.

But Ethelwulf did not notice this, having taken the letters eagerly from me, and broken open the first that came.

Now when he had read the first few lines, he looked up, and reading from the letter, which doubtless told him the names of the bearers-- "Heregar I know," he said; "which is Wulfhere?"

Then Wulfhere bowed, and the king asked for Wislac and Aldhelm, and then for each of the men in turn. And when each had answered, he looked hard at us, still holding the letter open, but saying nothing, and then fell to reading again. So we must stand still till all those letters were read.

Presently he took one, and reading the outside, gave it to the atheling, saying it was to him, and went on reading. That the atheling took, and as he read, looked at us, and it seemed particularly at me, though I thought nothing of that.

At last the king finished, and turned to a tall, noble-looking warrior who stood very near the dais, bidding him treat us with all honour, and see to our lodging near him while we were at court. Shortly, he said, he would speak to us of all we could tell him.

Then he held out his ungloved hand to us, which the atheling made a smiling sign for me to kiss, and that we all did, and then he looked pleasantly at us, and went his way from the hall, followed by his close attendants, with the queen and the atheling.

So soon as the king was gone, the talk began all over the hall, and most of all they crowded round us to learn what we could tell them; but that tall thane, whose name was Ceorle, came and took us away, telling the rest jestingly that they should have the second telling of the news, but that the king must have the first. And so he took us to guest chambers in his own house, and there left us in charge of his steward, treating us four thanes with all honour, and our men, as became their standing, among his own best men.

At least, this last was but for a short time, for the lay brethren came to me, looking oddly at me, and saying that they were in a strait; for, being lay brethren first, and warriors after, they knew not how to join in the talk and idle jests of the servants and housecarles. Moreover, they said that their vows obliged them to certain duties of prayer. And this I thought was honest of them, for many a lay brother would, when he found that I noted not their state, have broken out of bounds gladly, for the time.

So I sent for the steward, and asked him where they might be bestowed, and after a little thought, he said that the abbot, who had a following of honest house-carles, would take them in; and that he managed for us, and afterwards told me that Ealhstan's men had gained great praise, both for themselves and the bishop, by their ways in the abbey.

This is a little thing: but I tell it because it shows what sort of man Bishop Ealhstan was. For even over these rough warriors he had gained such a power for good that he had made of them all he wished--sturdy champions of the faith, both bodily and spiritually.

So when those three were gone elsewhere our only serving man was my collier, and well was he treated in Ceorle's house.

We bided quietly there all the rest of that day and that night, and then in the morning were bidden to speak with the king, Ceorle taking us four himself and sending one to find the lay brethren and Dudda.

The king sat with Alfred the Atheling in a private chamber, no other but Ceorle being beside him while we were there. And I was a little frightened about my putting aside the young prince now, for I knew who he was from Ceorle. But he had a pleasant look and greeting for us as we came in. So also had Ethelwulf himself, who seemed less stately than yesterday when he sat in his royal attire in full court.

Richly dressed he was now, with a gold circlet on his head and great gold bracelets on his arms; but he was in no high place, only sitting easily in a carved and cushioned chair, while the atheling sat on a settle by the window.

The letters I had brought lay open on the table at the king's elbow, and his hand was on them, and there were other writings scattered about; great ones with red seals hanging thereto--made no doubt by the gold signet which stood close by in its open casket.

"Come near, Thanes," the king said in his deep, quiet voice. "Let us talk together of this matter as friends, for a useless king were I but for such as you who keep my throne from the blows of enemies."

"Stay, Father," said Alfred the Atheling, starting up. "Let me write while the thanes speak," and he gathered up pens and such, and a roll of parchment, sitting down at the table and then holding pen ready, and looking at us.

The king smiled at him and his haste, and said, "Verily, Thanes, you must mind your words if Alfred writes them down, for he will ever keep records of tales such as yours, saying that they are for men to read hereafter."

But that had no terrors for us, seeing that we had a plain tale to tell, truth and nothing more. So, as Ceorle bid us, we four sat down by the window, and the king asked me to tell my story from the first.

So I began by saying that I had seen the landing of the Danes at Stert, and warned the watchmen of the levy.

There Alfred stopped me, holding up his pen suddenly.

"Tell us, Thane, of the Watchet landing," he said.

And when I began to tell of that he looked up again, with his eyes dancing, and asked me how I came on Quantock hill.

Thereat the king laughed a little, saying that Alfred should have been a law-man, and the atheling said that, with his father's help, he meant to be such, and a good one.

And that he has become, for the laws he has given us will last, as it seems to me, till the name of Saxon has departed.

Then I was a little in doubt what to say, and the king saw this. So he told me kindly that he had had very full accounts written by the bishop and ealdormen; but now both he and the atheling would fain hear about myself; that is, if my friends already knew all, and if I would not heed Ceorle.

Now I saw that I must speak more of myself than I wished, and would fain have been excused, saying something of that sort. But the atheling asked me to think of them as friends who would feel for me, saying, too, that of my own history he would not write, and so kindly did he urge me, drawing me on, that at last I had told him all from the beginning of my troubles, even to the time when I rode with Alswythe into Glastonbury and sought the bishop.

"That is well told," said Alfred, when I had finished so far, and the king sighed a little, but left all the speaking to his son.

"Now, Wulfhere," he went on, "it is your turn," and so made the old warrior take up the tale; but he bade him begin at the first fight.

However, Wulfhere must needs go back to the war arrow business, and then to the staying of the flight at Cannington, and in this Alfred did not stop him, though I thought it more than needed.

So he told all his tale, even to the slaying of the berserk, and things like that.

And as he told of the breaking of the ring, and our stand inside of it, Alfred the Atheling wrote fast, and presently he bade Wulfhere cease, and going to a corner took down a harp, while his father smiled on him, and tuning it, broke out into a wondrous war song that made our hearts beat fast, for we seemed to feel that it was full of the very shout and ring of battle inside our circle of foes, and we were as men who looked on and saw our own deeds over again, only made more glorious by the hand of the poet and the voice of the singer.

So that when he ended the king's eyes flashed, and Ceorle's face was red and good to look at with a war light on it, and Wislac shouted, as I had nearly done.

But at that sound, strange in the king's presence, we all started, and Wislac seemed abashed.

"Truly, Lord King," he said humbly, "I could not help it."

"Almost had I done as you did," said the kindly king. "Alfred must bear the blame. Now shall you tell your story."

But Wislac said he had nought to add to Wulfhere's tale, save that Aldhelm here had saved him at his own cost, and that he had had, moreover, as much fighting as he was like ever to want.

But even from him Alfred gained many things about the fighting, and from Aldhelm also, and these he wrote down.

Thus we all told our tales, and they were long in the telling, so that when Aldhelm had finished, the king rose up, blaming Alfred gently for the long sitting, saying, however, that he had feared somewhat of the sort, but that doubtless the thanes were more wearied than either of the other three who had listened.

"Now," he said, "well have you four thanes deserved of me and of all, and you shall not say that the king is ungrateful. And I think that each of you has said less of your own selves than might be said, or, indeed, than is said in these letters. Now have Ceorle and I and my council spoken of this matter, and we have thought of rewards fitting for the shield wall of the standard."

Then would we thank the king; but he bade us wait for a little, putting his hand on those great parchments with the seals. One of these he took and gave to Aldhelm.

"This is to your father, confirming his rights of the land he holds of me to him and his heirs for ever, by reason of your good service. Yet is there a little blame to you from the way in which you found a foremost place, though much praise for the holding thereof and in your manner of ending that quarrel."

So Aldhelm took the deed and kissed the king's hand in token of homage, going to his place very glad, for this was what his father desired most of all.

Then the king beckoned Wislac and gave him also a deed like Aldhelm's, granting him the lordship of the manor of Goring on the Thames, and that was a good reward to the stout Mercian, who thanked the king, saying that he wotted not how his majesty knew what he would have most wished. Whereupon the king laughed, saying that kings knew more than men gave them credit for, and so Wislac did homage, and sat down.

Then Ethelwulf looked at Wulfhere, and said; "Wulfhere, my old warrior, I know not rightly what to do with you, for you are a lonely man, and I think that a place in my court would not suit you. Nor would you care to hold a manor in a strange place. Wait a little, and we will think it over."

Now at that Wulfhere looked glad, for I think he feared rather than desired reward.

Now came my turn, and my face flushed, and I was a little frightened, for there was but one thing I wanted, and I feared that that might not be.

But the king made a step towards me and took me by the hand, looking hard at me.

"Heregar," he said, "yours has been a strange story, and from beginning to end you have been first in this victory that will gain us peace for many years to come. Moreover you have suffered wrong, being punished for evil falsely laid to your charge on my account. And that I must show all men to be untrue, and that I, the king, hold it so. Now shall you choose your own reward."

Then was I sorely abashed, not knowing how to say what I longed for, and the king stood waiting a little. And maybe I should never have got it out, but the atheling looked up, and said:

"May I speak for you, Heregar?"

And so plainly did I see that he knew all, that I asked him to do so, and he came beside me and said; "Heregar needs but one thing, my father, and that is the hand of the maiden he loves--Alswythe the daughter of Matelgar, and your ward since her father was slain."

"Are you so foolish as to ask no more than that?" said the king, smiling.

And on that my tongue was loosed, and I answered; "Aye my Lord the King. If foolish it be to long for the one whom a man loves, and who loves him, so that he holds her beyond all other reward."

"Then is your request granted," said the king very kindly. "Yet must you have withal to keep so great a treasure rightly."

Now I had forgotten that I was landless, and well it was for me that the king went on quickly; "So I give you the lands that were Matelgar's, and your own lands again; and my men, and at my cost, shall build your halls afresh that the Danes have burnt. And whatever rights were Matelgar's or your father's shall be confirmed to you and yours for ever. Yet these things are but justice, and no reward."

So he paused a little, and I found courage to speak.

"My Lord the King, I need no more than you have given, for love and honour and lands have come back to me, and withal friendship of these three here, and of Ealhstan the Bishop, and of the noble ealdormen; while but for what has befallen I might have been still a careless thane, living at ease and for naught; but now, having heard Your good words, it is enough, and reward fit for any man."

And this I meant from my heart, for no more could I see that any man should need than this: honour of his fellows and of the king, and love and lands, and friends. Surely is a man rich in these things.

Yet must Alfred the Atheling add a word.

"Call me your friend also, Heregar, if you will, for fain would I be so," and he held out his strong white hand to take mine.

And it is good to think that, as it were, the grasp of his has never slackened from that day to this, but that he is my friend still.

Then Ceorle must say likewise, and last of all the king said; "Friend to all my people would I be, and to none more than to those who have risked life for the land. Therefore, to you and yours am I friend always, so that you shall ever think of me as friend first and king after. Nor is it to everyone that I dare say that, Heregar, my friend."

And he took my hand also, as the atheling and Ceorle had taken it.

So was I fain to weep for very joy at all this that had come to me, and must turn away for a little lest it should be seen.

Then the king spoke cheerfully, as on business.

"Now, Heregar, I have work for you to do in your home; for I would have no man idle. Here is Watchet town burnt up, and no man left--for its lord is slain--to see that it is built aright, and that each man, or family, has his own again. Now, you knew that place well, nor is it very far from you. Therefore shall you see to all that, and you shall have writings from me to back you. But men must know that you yourself have power there, and, therefore, I make you lord of all Quantock side, from Watchet stream to Parret, and from the borders of your own land at Cannington to Severn shore between those two. And this shall you render in return for those rights: that you shall be ready at all times to bear the standard of Wessex, against all comers from over seas, at my bidding."

Now that was the Dragon of Wessex of which the old witch spoke. And lo! those things that had been foretold of me were sooth, and I knelt before the king, and swore to bear him this service faithfully.

So the rest bore witness of that oath gladly, rejoicing in the honour, which was in truth to them as well as to me, for I could not have gone through aught without them, and if mine was the grip on Ealhstan's banner shaft, theirs were the hands that had kept it there.

Then said Ethelwulf; "Choose now one who shall have charge under you of the watchings and beacons on your shore."

And straightway I turned to Wulfhere, and begged him to do this for me, and it was good to see the warrior's face light up with gladness as he promised to give me his help. Doubtless that was what the king had in store for him, for at once he gave him the manor of the Watchet thane who had been slain, for as it chanced he had no heirs, and the land came back to the king.

That was the end of a long morning's work, and very kindly did Ethelwulf take his leave of us, saying that we must have these matters confirmed when the Witan [xii] met in two days' time.

So we went out, landed men and noble, and with us went the atheling, who took us to his own lodgings at the abbey, where he would see and speak to our men that he might write yet more from their lips, for he said that often it was good to hear what the common sort thought.

And my collier must needs tell him--for he was very pleasant, so that none need fear his rank--of Grendel, and also of the saint, which mightily pleased the atheling. So that often would he call me "Grendel" in sport thereafter, for we grew close friends in the time we bided at Salisbury.

And that seemed long to me, for now would I fain be back at Glastonbury with Alswythe.

Soon Wislac, also, grew tired of the court, and said that he longed for the deep meadows and lofty trees, and green downs along the clear river in this June time, and must seek his own home again. But it seemed that Alfred over-persuaded him, for reasons which he told me not, and he stayed.

We went to the great meeting of the Witan, taking our seats there when our rights were confirmed to us. And into my hands was put the standard of Wessex by the king himself, and I bore it to the great church, there to be blessed in the bearing thereof.

And there stood Ealhstan himself in his robes, having come even that morning for this very purpose. And that was pleasant, and even as I should have most wished. Moreover, my friends, and Alfred, and Ceorle stood by me as if for shield wall at that time, and I was well attended.

Now betimes, in the afternoon, came Alfred the Atheling to me as I sat with Ceorle, talking of the arms of the vikings, and asked me to come and speak with friends of his, who would not see him save he brought me.

And at that Ceorle laughed, saying that they must be of importance if they would deny the prince an audience, making conditions. And Alfred said very gravely that they were so, and maybe the only people, save the king and queen, who might delay seeing him.

So I was curious to know who these were. But we left Ceorle still laughing. Then Alfred took me to the abbey, and sent one of his men to say we had come, who, when he returned, bade us into the presence of these people.

When we came to a great door, in a part of the abbey where I had not before been, he took my arm, and pushed me in first, saying that he would ensure himself a good reception; and there sat Ealhstan, and beside him stood Alswythe, smiling at me, and with a little colour in her face.

CHAPTER XVIII. PEACE IN THE LAND.

Now of the wedding in the great church I knew very little, save that I had Alswythe beside me, and that Ealhstan married us. And that was all I cared for, heeding naught of the rest.

But the king and the queen were there, and many thanes, while the atheling must needs be a groomsman with my friends, and Ceorle gave away the bride on the king's behalf. There, too, was Eanulf, looking very noble in his court array, beside the king. And the little page in blue and silver who held Alswythe's dress was none other than Turkil, "Grendel's friend" as Alfred called him, whom Alswythe had begged the bishop to bring with him.

There also was Dudda the Collier, clad beyond knowledge by Wislac, holding my helm and sword, and the lay brethren, mail clad for the last time, with the white cross painted on their shields and helms. Lustily did they join in the chanting.

Osric only was not there, but on Alswythe's neck and arms shone presently wonderfully-wrought collar and bracelets of gold that he had sent, having had them made from the spoils of that tall viking chief that I had slain.

Then was there feasting, and songs of gleemen, and, better still, that song of Stert fight sung by Alfred the Atheling himself in full hall. And then had Wislac full excuse for what he did in the king's presence, for at the end all the hall joined in a mighty Wessex war shout. And that, said the atheling, was a poet's greatest praise, to have stirred the hearts of men to forgetfulness of aught but the song.

Now, when we must needs ride away westward, with Wulfhere and Aldhelm for attendants, and the collier and my lay brethren again for guards, the king gave Alswythe a ring, praying her to spare me to him if need should be; and she, half weeping, yet proudly, told him that she would be the first to arm me for his service. And the queen kissed her, but the atheling said that soon he should see us again, for he would ride with me over the battle-ground, and learn it all, when our hall was ready for a guest.

Then Wislac took leave of us last of all, even as we started, for he said he would have no long leave taking. Nor did he know if he must not come with Alfred to fight the battle over again. And we prayed him to do so, for I loved the quaint sayings and cool valour of the broad-shouldered thane.

But Eanulf and Ceorle rode with many of the thanes a mile or more with us on our way from the town, and there, having set us fairly off, left us with hearty good-speeds. But they left one behind, who joined himself to our little company. And that was Turkil, clad like myself in silver mail, and on a white pony, but with flame-coloured cloak and scarf. For that was the atheling's doing, when he knew that "Grendel's friend" was to be brought up in our hall, to grow into the stout warrior I had boded him to be.

Now should my story be ended were it a fairy tale, but it is not that. Well I knew that, happy as I was, the day must come when I must bear forward to battle the golden dragon banner of Wessex, and I cannot rightly tell if I dreaded or longed for that day. Maybe there was a mixture of both dread and longing in my thoughts thereof.

But when we came over Brent Knoll, on our way back to my place and Alswythe's at Cannington, there lay the black ships under the holms yet, and there, too, were the burnt walls of our houses, though these were rising up again as the king's men wrought at them. And all the land lay waste and neglected, and, as we rode over Cannington hill, a broken helm rolled from my horse's hoof from among the grass of the roadside. Those things brought back to us the memory of war and trouble even in our new happiness; and there, over the river, was the new-made mound over Elgar, the man who had died for his land, and not in vain.

It was many days since we started from Salisbury town, however, before we came to Cannington, and in that time we had sought the house of Turkil's father, the franklin, lodging with him for a day and night, that we might seek Leofwine the hermit. But him we might not find, for he was dead, and that grieved me sorely, for I would fain have seen him again, aye, and if it might be, taken him to live with us.

But he died as the tide went out on the day of Stert fight, and those who stood by him say that he had visions of all that befell there.

For many times he called to me as exhorting me; and once, after long silence, in the gray of early dawn, he rose up, crying, "Up, Ealhstan, up, for the Lord has delivered these heathen into your hands!"

And that was at the time when the bishop had heard those words spoken to him. And again, once more he roused, even at the time when the Danes drew off from us at the coming of Osric. He lifted his hands, crying "Victory!" thrice, and then saying very softly, "Heregar, my son," was silent thereafter till he died at the time of the lowest ebb, only his lips moving as if in prayer. And I remembered the strange voice I had heard crying round me, and I wept, for I thought how much more was wrought by the prayers of feeble ones than men wot of.

But his prophecy had indeed come true, and though I might not see him more, the memory of Leofwine is with me always, with his words of wise counsel that he had spoken to me.

Now of that other one who prophesied in her strange way to me I know no more, nor did I ever see her again. Gundred the witch, men called her, knowing her well, and fearing her. But she was never seen after the Danes swept over our land, and how she ended none ever knew. I sought her carefully that I might give her shelter and ease for the rest of her days, but without avail.

All his life long has Dudda the Collier bided with me, serving well and roughly, but in all most faithfully, as is his wont. And not many days after we came homewards he brought me the berserk's axe to hang in hall, for he had taken it and hidden it when we left the battlefield on the day after the fight. So there it is now, and beside it hangs the raven flag of the largest ship, for he must needs go with the fishers across to the holms, and bring me back the tale of how the last of the Danes had perished.

And now what am I to say of the years since our hall was built again? Long have they been, and not all happy, for many a time have I had to bear the standard of Wessex against the Danes. Yet Stert fight won us six years of peace, and after that the Earl Ceorle and I led our levies and conquered at Wenbury. But that was Wulfhere's last fight, for of his wounds he might not recover, though we bore him back and tended him carefully for a month or more. So he lies in God's Acre at Cannington, and is at rest.

Then came long years of fighting, and ever I bore the banner, and ever Alswythe set me forth most lovingly, with brave words that should bide with me till I came back to her. And all the time our hall was safe, for beyond Parret the Danes came not again.

And to tell of all those fights were too long, or of how Wislac and Aldhelm would ever fight beside me as of old, and at last Turkil in Aldhelm's place, when that brave thane fell at Wilton, fighting for Alfred the King.

Then were we in Athelney with Alfred, and it was the collier who found us that place of safety. And thence we went at last to victory again, and now once more the land has rest.

Yet Wislac is with us in Wulfhere's place, for his own land is in Danish hands, and we know not what wars may be yet with them, though we have stood by the king's side when the greatest victory of all was won, and Guthrum the heathen became Athelstan the Christian, and peaceful division of the land was made.

So I and Alswythe grow old here in Cannington, seeing our children grow up around us. And Alfred the king has our eldest in his court, there training him in all things well and wisely. And Turkil is thane of Watchet, and our son-in-law, much loved by all, well and faithfully tending all my shore as Wulfhere tended it in his time.

So to me and mine after storm has come peace, and with us and the land all is well.

THE END.

i A representative assembly or court of judgment.

ii An outlaw for whose slaying there was a reward, or at least no penalty.

iii A curved, one-edged sword or war knife.

iv The "Saga of Beowulf" was the great popular poem of the Saxon races, and as well known to them as the legends of Robin Hood to us. The principal episode is the hero's victory over the marsh fiend Grendel.

v Crowland in Lincolnshire, where the saint founded his monastery.

vi Like the Highland "fiery cross", the signal for rising in arms.

vii The most contemptuous term that could be applied to a Saxon. Its exact force is lost, but may be expressed by "worth nothing."

viii The border of cleared land round a forest settlement, across which in times of war none might come without sound of horn in warning.

ix The "Saga of Beowulf" as we have it is the work of a Christian editor of King Alfred's time.

x A corselet or coat of mail.

xi The bell which is rung during mass.

xii The great national council, or parliament.

The Codes Of Hammurabi And Moses
W. W. Davies

QTY

The discovery of the Hammurabi Code is one of the greatest achievements of archaeology, and is of paramount interest, not only to the student of the Bible, but also to all those interested in ancient history...

Religion   **ISBN:** *1-59462-338-4*   **Pages:132**
MSRP $12.95

The Theory of Moral Sentiments
Adam Smith

QTY

This work from 1749. contains original theories of conscience amd moral judgment and it is the foundation for systemof morals.

Philosophy   **ISBN:** *1-59462-777-0*   **Pages:536**
MSRP $19.95

Jessica's First Prayer
Hesba Stretton

QTY

In a screened and secluded corner of one of the many railway-bridges which span the streets of London there could be seen a few years ago, from five o'clock every morning until half past eight, a tidily set-out coffee-stall, consisting of a trestle and board, upon which stood two large tin cans, with a small fire of charcoal burning under each so as to keep the coffee boiling during the early hours of the morning when the work-people were thronging into the city on their way to their daily toil...

Childrens   **ISBN:** *1-59462-373-2*   **Pages:84**
MSRP $9.95

My Life and Work
Henry Ford

QTY

Henry Ford revolutionized the world with his implementation of mass production for the Model T automobile. Gain valuable business insight into his life and work with his own auto-biography... "We have only started on our development of our country we have not as yet, with all our talk of wonderful progress, done more than scratch the surface. The progress has been wonderful enough but..."

Biographies/   **ISBN:** *1-59462-198-5*   **Pages:300**
MSRP $21.95

The Art of Cross-Examination
Francis Wellman

QTY

I presume it is the experience of every author, after his first book is published upon an important subject, to be almost overwhelmed with a wealth of ideas and illustrations which could readily have been included in his book, and which to his own mind, at least, seem to make a second edition inevitable. Such certainly was the case with me; and when the first edition had reached its sixth impression in five months, I rejoiced to learn that it seemed to my publishers that the book had met with a sufficiently favorable reception to justify a second and considerably enlarged edition. ..

Reference   **ISBN:** *1-59462-647-2*

Pages:412

MSRP $19.95

On the Duty of Civil Disobedience
Henry David Thoreau

QTY

Thoreau wrote his famous essay, On the Duty of Civil Disobedience, as a protest against an unjust but popular war and the immoral but popular institution of slave-owning. He did more than write—he declined to pay his taxes, and was hauled off to gaol in consequence. Who can say how much this refusal of his hastened the end of the war and of slavery ?

Law   **ISBN:** *1-59462-747-9*

Pages:48

MSRP $7.45

Dream Psychology Psychoanalysis for Beginners
Sigmund Freud

QTY

Sigmund Freud, born Sigismund Schlomo Freud (May 6, 1856 - September 23, 1939), was a Jewish-Austrian neurologist and psychiatrist who co-founded the psychoanalytic school of psychology. Freud is best known for his theories of the unconscious mind, especially involving the mechanism of repression; his redefinition of sexual desire as mobile and directed towards a wide variety of objects; and his therapeutic techniques, especially his understanding of transference in the therapeutic relationship and the presumed value of dreams as sources of insight into unconscious desires.

Dream Psychology
Psychoanalysis for Beginners

Sigmund Freud

Psychology   **ISBN:** *1-59462-905-6*

Pages:196

MSRP $15.45

The Miracle of Right Thought
Orison Swett Marden

QTY

Believe with all of your heart that you will do what you were made to do. When the mind has once formed the habit of holding cheerful, happy, prosperous pictures, it will not be easy to form the opposite habit. It does not matter how improbable or how far away this realization may see, or how dark the prospects may be, if we visualize them as best we can, as vividly as possible, hold tenaciously to them and vigorously struggle to attain them, they will gradually become actualized, realized in the life. But a desire, a longing without endeavor, a yearning abandoned or held indifferently will vanish without realization.

Self Help   **ISBN:** *1-59462-644-8*

Pages:360

MSRP $25.45

The Rosicrucian Cosmo-Conception Mystic Christianity *by Max Heindel* ISBN: *1-59462-188-8* **$38.95**
The Rosicrucian Cosmo-conception is not dogmatic, neither does it appeal to any other authority than the reason of the student. It is: not controversial, but is: sent forth in the, hope that it may help to clear... New Age/Religion Pages 646

Abandonment To Divine Providence *by Jean-Pierre de Caussade* ISBN: *1-59462-228-0* **$25.95**
"The Rev. Jean Pierre de Caussade was one of the most remarkable spiritual writers of the Society of Jesus in France in the 18th Century. His death took place at Toulouse in 1751. His works have gone through many editions and have been republished... Inspirational/Religion Pages 400

Mental Chemistry *by Charles Haanel* ISBN: *1-59462-192-6* **$23.95**
Mental Chemistry allows the change of material conditions by combining and appropriately utilizing the power of the mind. Much like applied chemistry creates something new and unique out of careful combinations of chemicals the mastery of mental chemistry... New Age Pages 354

The Letters of Robert Browning and Elizabeth Barret Barrett 1845-1846 vol II ISBN: *1-59462-193-4* **$35.95**
by Robert Browning and Elizabeth Barrett Biographies Pages 596

Gleanings In Genesis (volume I) *by Arthur W. Pink* ISBN: *1-59462-130-6* **$27.45**
Appropriately has Genesis been termed "the seed plot of the Bible" for in it we have, in germ form, almost all of the great doctrines which are afterwards fully developed in the books of Scripture which follow... Religion/Inspirational Pages 420

The Master Key *by L. W. de Laurence* ISBN: *1-59462-001-6* **$30.95**
In no branch of human knowledge has there been a more lively increase of the spirit of research during the past few years than in the study of Psychology, Concentration and Mental Discipline. The requests for authentic lessons in Thought Control, Mental Discipline and... New Age/Business Pages 422

The Lesser Key Of Solomon Goetia *by L. W. de Laurence* ISBN: *1-59462-092-X* **$9.95**
This translation of the first book of the "Lernegton" which is now for the first time made accessible to students of Talismanic Magic was done, after careful collation and edition, from numerous Ancient Manuscripts in Hebrew, Latin, and French... New Age/Occult Pages 92

Rubaiyat Of Omar Khayyam *by Edward Fitzgerald* ISBN:*1-59462-332-5* **$13.95**
Edward Fitzgerald, whom the world has already learned, in spite of his own efforts to remain within the shadow of anonymity, to look upon as one of the rarest poets of the century, was born at Bredfield, in Suffolk, on the 31st of March, 1809. He was the third son of John Purcell... Music Pages 172

Ancient Law *by Henry Maine* ISBN: *1-59462-128-4* **$29.95**
The chief object of the following pages is to indicate some of the earliest ideas of mankind, as they are reflected in Ancient Law, and to point out the relation of those ideas to modern thought. Religiuon/History Pages 452

Far-Away Stories *by William J. Locke* ISBN: *1-59462-129-2* **$19.45**
"Good wine needs no bush, but a collection of mixed vintages does. And this book is just such a collection. Some of the stories I do not want to remain buried for ever in the museum files of dead magazine-numbers an author's not unpardonable vanity..." Fiction Pages 272

Life of David Crockett *by David Crockett* ISBN: *1-59462-250-7* **$27.45**
"Colonel David Crockett was one of the most remarkable men of the times in which he lived. Born in humble life, but gifted with a strong will, an indomitable courage, and unremitting perseverance... Biographies/New Age Pages 424

Lip-Reading *by Edward Nitchie* ISBN: *1-59462-206-X* **$25.95**
Edward B. Nitchie, founder of the New York School for the Hard of Hearing, now the Nitchie School of Lip-Reading, Inc, wrote "LIP-READING Principles and Practice". The development and perfecting of this meritorious work on lip-reading was an undertaking... How-to Pages 400

A Handbook of Suggestive Therapeutics, Applied Hypnotism, Psychic Science ISBN: *1-59462-214-0* **$24.95**
by Henry Munro Health/New Age/Health/Self-help Pages 376

A Doll's House: and Two Other Plays *by Henrik Ibsen* ISBN: *1-59462-112-8* **$19.95**
Henrik Ibsen created this classic when in revolutionary 1848 Rome. Introducing some striking concepts in playwriting for the realist genre, this play has been studied the world over. Fiction/Classics/Plays 308

The Light of Asia *by sir Edwin Arnold* ISBN: *1-59462-204-3* **$13.95**
In this poetic masterpiece, Edwin Arnold describes the life and teachings of Buddha. The man who was to become known as Buddha to the world was born as Prince Gautama of India but he rejected the worldly riches and abandoned the reigns of power when... Religion/History/Biographies Pages 170

The Complete Works of Guy de Maupassant *by Guy de Maupassant* ISBN: *1-59462-157-8* **$16.95**
"For days and days, nights and nights, I had dreamed of that first kiss which was to consecrate our engagement, and I knew not on what spot I should put my lips..." Fiction/Classics Pages 240

The Art of Cross-Examination *by Francis L. Wellman* ISBN: *1-59462-309-0* **$26.95**
Written by a renowned trial lawyer, Wellman imparts his experience and uses case studies to explain how to use psychology to extract desired information through questioning. How-to/Science/Reference Pages 408

Answered or Unanswered? *by Louisa Vaughan* ISBN: *1-59462-248-5* **$10.95**
Miracles of Faith in China Religion Pages 112

The Edinburgh Lectures on Mental Science (1909) *by Thomas* ISBN: *1-59462-008-3* **$11.95**
This book contains the substance of a course of lectures recently given by the writer in the Queen Street Hail, Edinburgh. Its purpose is to indicate the Natural Principles governing the relation between Mental Action and Material Conditions... New Age/Psychology Pages 148

Ayesha *by H. Rider Haggard* ISBN: *1-59462-301-5* **$24.95**
Verily and indeed it is the unexpected that happens! Probably if there was one person upon the earth from whom the Editor of this, and of a certain previous history, did not expect to hear again... Classics Pages 380

Ayala's Angel *by Anthony Trollope* ISBN: *1-59462-352-X* **$29.95**
The two girls were both pretty, but Lucy who was twenty-one who supposed to be simple and comparatively unattractive, whereas Ayala was credited, as her Bombwhat romantic name might show, with poetic charm and a taste for romance. Ayala when her father died was nineteen... Fiction Pages 484

The American Commonwealth *by James Bryce* ISBN: *1-59462-286-8* **$34.45**
An interpretation of American democratic political theory. It examines political mechanics and society from the perspective of Scotsman James Bryce Politics Pages 572

Stories of the Pilgrims *by Margaret P. Pumphrey* ISBN: *1-59462-116-0* **$17.95**
This book explores pilgrims religious oppression in England as well as their escape to Holland and eventual crossing to America on the Mayflower, and their early days in New England... History Pages 268

www.bookjungle.com *email: sales@bookjungle.com fax: 630-214-0564 mail: Book Jungle PO Box 2226 Champaign, IL 61825*

QTY

The Fasting Cure by *Sinclair Upton*   ISBN: *1-59462-222-1*   **$13.95**
In the Cosmopolitan Magazine for May, 1910, and in the Contemporary Review (London) for April, 1910, I published an article dealing with my experiences in fasting. I have written a great many magazine articles, but never one which attracted so much attention... New Age/Self Help/Health Pages 164

Hebrew Astrology by *Sepharial*   ISBN: *1-59462-308-2*   **$13.45**
In these days of advanced thinking it is a matter of common observation that we have left many of the old landmarks behind and that we are now pressing forward to greater heights and to a wider horizon than that which represented the mind-content of our progenitors... Astrology Pages 144

Thought Vibration or The Law of Attraction in the Thought World   ISBN: *1-59462-127-6*   **$12.95**
by *William Walker Atkinson*   *Psychology/Religion Pages 144*

Optimism by *Helen Keller*   ISBN: *1-59462-108-X*   **$15.95**
Helen Keller was blind, deaf, and mute since 19 months old, yet famously learned how to overcome these handicaps, communicate with the world, and spread her lectures promoting optimism. An inspiring read for everyone... Biographies/Inspirational Pages 84

Sara Crewe by *Frances Burnett*   ISBN: *1-59462-360-0*   **$9.45**
In the first place, Miss Minchin lived in London. Her home was a large, dull, tall one, in a large, dull square, where all the houses were alike, and all the sparrows were alike, and where all the door-knockers made the same heavy sound... Childrens/Classic Pages 88

The Autobiography of Benjamin Franklin by *Benjamin Franklin*   ISBN: *1-59462-135-7*   **$24.95**
The Autobiography of Benjamin Franklin has probably been more extensively read than any other American historical work, and no other book of its kind has had such ups and downs of fortune. Franklin lived for many years in England, where he was agent... Biographies/History Pages 332

Name	
Email	
Telephone	
Address	
City, State ZIP	

☐ **Credit Card**   ☐ **Check / Money Order**

Credit Card Number	
Expiration Date	
Signature	

Please Mail to: Book Jungle
                              PO Box 2226
                              Champaign, IL 61825
or Fax to: 630-214-0564

ORDERING INFORMATION

web: *www.bookjungle.com*
email: *sales@bookjungle.com*
fax: *630-214-0564*
mail: *Book Jungle PO Box 2226 Champaign, IL 61825*
or PayPal *to sales@bookjungle.com*

Please contact us for bulk discounts

DIRECT-ORDER TERMS

**20% Discount if You Order
Two or More Books**
Free Domestic Shipping!
Accepted: Master Card, Visa,
Discover, American Express